Black American Psycho

Psycho

A Novel

Ernest Baker

ISBN: 1535277475
ISBN-13: 978-1535277471

DEDICATION

To my wife and daughter.

CONTENTS

DISCLAIMER

ONE

Leslie Nostril hit Arthur Simon for the first time on New Year's Eve. They were in Buffalo, New York. They were supposed to be celebrating the end of a difficult year.

The blow landed on Arthur's face six minutes before midnight. He recoiled from the assault, held both hands to his right temple, and cursed Leslie's name.

Leslie, whose tiny frame did not match her capacity for violence, laughed furiously. Condensation escaped a mouth stained by too much red wine. The final moon of 2013 reflected off the cheap leather of her jacket.

Abuse entered the fray of Arthur and Leslie's relationship. Abuse would define their union.

Eight months before Leslie punched Arthur, Arthur moved to Los Angeles for a new job.

When Arthur left New York that spring, he and Leslie had been dating for two months and having sex for a year. They kept the relationship secret because Leslie was Arthur's intern at *Abstract* magazine.

They were both twenty-four years old. The potential scandal was not about age.

Arthur and Leslie kept the relationship secret because Leslie needed *Abstract* to take her seriously.

She had already slept with the social editor at the magazine. The editor-in-chief of *Abstract*, Boris Craven, warned Arthur that his fraternization with Leslie was ruining her chances of being hired.

But Leslie was hired. Her master's degree and strong work ethic were to credit, though Arthur did a significant amount of lobbying on her behalf.

"Tell Boris I deserve full-time," Leslie would say to Arthur. "Vouch for me."

And so, in the months leading up to Leslie's hire, Arthur campaigned.

He stressed Leslie's competence in meetings. He emphasized her contributions over drinks. The plot was a practice in persistence. Every time Arthur mentioned Leslie during *Abstract* business, Boris smirked with the critical glare of an unsold superior.

With enough tenacity on Arthur's part, and mounting proficiency on Leslie's, the tactic eventually worked. Leslie got the assistant editor title and a thirty thousand dollar salary.

Before they could bask in the afterglow of her accomplishment, Arthur relocated to the other side of the country and left Leslie to fend for herself in the city.

Arthur and Leslie's first year of knowing one another was filled with unsafe sex and illicit drugs.

MDMA was their drug of choice. Sometimes they took it twice in a weekend, living out the high on the green sofa in Arthur's East Williamsburg apartment, waves of euphoria reverberating throughout their adjacent bodies.

Leslie fell in love quickly. She was afflicted with a burning desire for Arthur from the moment they began hooking up during his final weeks in Harlem. She ignored insistent pleas for sex from previous suitors.

Arthur, however, took advantage of the liberties accompanying their lack of exclusivity.

Over Thanksgiving break of that first year, Arthur slept with music writer Maggie Harvey when he went home to Chicago.

Within minutes of meeting at her Logan Square apartment, after mouthfuls of cognac and an overstuffed blunt, Arthur was in Maggie's bed. His hands grazed her half-shaved head when she went down on him. His body pressed against her pale, tattooed skin with each thrust.

Then they did it again at Christmas.

Maggie would go on to become close friends with Leslie and play a crucial role in Arthur Simon's demise, but that was not yet apparent.

When Arthur and Leslie returned to New York after the holidays, she pressed him for a commitment. Arthur was reluctant, and viewed Leslie as more of a friend with benefits than a girlfriend, but: MDMA.

And so, on an icy February night, after an hour of listening to *1017 Thug* while rolling face, Arthur and Leslie made it official. Their favorite bar, the Graham, was the scene of the crime.

"I love you," she said, "but I can't do this anymore if I'm not your girlfriend."

"So be my girlfriend," he said, "and I'll be your boyfriend. That's fine."

Arthur wanted to keep his single man charade going forever, but he knew that he loved her too. Or loved things about her. Falling in love on drugs is easy.

Arthur and Leslie's habits did not mesh well with their responsibilities at *Abstract*.

Leslie was weeks away from becoming a staff member. Arthur had been promoted. Boris and his most loyal comrade, Johnny Pearson, the magazine's strategist, were relentless about web traffic.

Arthur hit the traffic goals ordained to him, but he found the work trite and unfulfilling. By April, he was interviewing for a copywriter position at Sounds by Surgeon Tre, a Los Angeles-based company best known for its expensive headphones.

"They offered me a job," said Arthur, sitting next to Leslie at Kellogg's Diner, after the interview.

"Are you going to take it?" she asked.

"Yes," said Arthur. "I leave in two weeks. I've always wanted to live in California."

"What does that mean for us?" said Leslie, narrowing her eyes, barely concealing her contempt for Arthur's impulsive decision.

A week later, when Boris, Johnny, and two more of *Abstract*'s top editors brought Arthur into a secluded office to reprimand him for his inconsistent performance, he told them that their criticism was no longer necessary.

Arthur and Leslie broke up to avoid the complications of long-distance relationships.

Tears streamed down her face as Arthur's cab raced towards LaGuardia.

Los Angeles was a short-lived affair.

During Arthur's eight months in the city, his, and, more so, Leslie's indiscretions with others were limited compared to the promiscuity of which each was capable.

Arthur slept with an ex-girlfriend from Chicago, a female co-worker, a male neighbor, a famous novelist's boyfriend, one Twitter user from Toronto, and another from Oklahoma City, Eleanor London—a young, thin brunette infatuated with the Internet fame Arthur had earned from a streak of successful music articles.

Leslie slept with an ex-boyfriend from Buffalo.

Arthur and Leslie spoke daily. Arthur visited Leslie in New York often. He purchased flights on Friday nights just to spend thirty-six hours in the city with her.

On those trips to New York, Arthur rediscovered his love for the city. He was affected with an encroaching sense of possessiveness towards Leslie.

She, too, had burned out at *Abstract*, and, with the help of a reference from Arthur, took a part-time position at *Lice*, a competing outlet that covered music in a manner both wry and, occasionally, offensive.

When Arthur was in Los Angeles, Leslie spent her time with her *Lice* co-workers Pooh Dillard and Derek Blubbermann. Pooh was a skinny white boy from North Carolina. Derek was a chubby white boy from Iowa.

When Arthur was in New York, the four of them sat around in dingy Brooklyn apartments snorting cocaine, drinking, and gossiping. Arthur saw how Leslie had become entangled in Pooh and Derek's affairs. He felt like he was losing her. He was.

Arthur had a plan.

He could afford to quit his job in Los Angeles. For the first time in Arthur's life, the balance on his checking account read five digits. Leslie's rent was only twelve hundred dollars per month.

Arthur was lonely in Los Angeles. His loneliness was why his writing gained traction that year. He had the freedom to write with a feverish determination because he was not as romantically successful as he had envisioned.

Arthur had always gotten laid with a respectable consistency, but he was never one of those guys who could take someone home every night of the week.

Leslie became Arthur's best option. They were dating again by autumn. Getting back together had the opposite intended effect and drove them further apart.

Leslie spent more time with Pooh and Derek and answered fewer calls from Arthur.

Arthur's suspicions peaked when Leslie did not answer his calls on Halloween.

He got Leslie's voicemail for the seventeenth time that day. He saw a photo on Twitter of Leslie with Pooh, Derek, and Maggie. (Maggie had moved to Brooklyn.)

Arthur sat alone in a vacant parking lot on Fairfax Avenue and sobbed to "Satellite of Love."

The next time Arthur visited Leslie, he slit his left wrist to the white meat when Leslie discovered that he was still talking to his ex-girlfriend from Chicago.

Arthur reconnected with his ex because he craved the attention that he no longer got from Leslie.

Slitting his wrist was an act of desperation carried out to cope with the three thousand mile distance.

Arthur lost his mind all alone on the other side of the country. The thick pools of crimson blood on Leslie's floor were a testament to that.

"You tried to kill yourself in my kitchen," Leslie said, over the phone the following week, smoking a cigarette outside of the *Lice* office on North Eleventh Street. "If you come back, you need to get help."

"I'm going somewhere tonight," said Arthur, fingering the inconspicuous athletic tape on his left arm.

That night, Arthur attended a therapy session at Southern California Counseling Center.

The next day, Arthur told his boss at Sounds by Surgeon Tre that he was moving back to New York.

A week before Christmas, Pooh and Leslie did MDMA in Pooh's apartment on Fayette Street. Leslie told Arthur that she was going to crash on Pooh's couch.

Leslie called Arthur in the middle of the night. Her voice trembled. She woke up to Pooh kissing her.

Pooh's girlfriend, Tina Alvarez, came home to Los Angeles, for the holidays, the next night. She wanted to meet up with Arthur.

Arthur and Tina had exchanged basic flirtations before—semi-risqué selfies, a "wouldn't it be better if we were dating each other" energy to their conversations. Arthur knew revenge was possible.

They went to a nightclub in Hollywood. They sat in the VIP section. They drank vodka. They gawked at celebrities. They danced. They drank more vodka.

They held hands as Tina led Arthur out of the nightclub and back to his car.

Revenge.

Tina removed her heels and washed off her makeup in Arthur's en suite bathroom.

In bed, they started on separate sides of the mattress but slowly moved closer. Tina pushed her body against Arthur's. Arthur burrowed his face into her neck.

He drove her to Venice in the morning.

All of that was in the past.

Arthur moved back to New York for Leslie. They began their new life together on New Year's Eve.

Arthur danced with Leslie in the Nostril family's kitchen at 11:00 p.m. The night took a turn for the worse when they met up with Leslie's hometown friends.

Leslie's friends scrambled to get to the bars in time for the countdown. They put on their coats and filed outside to the two cars available.

Leslie's friends did not account for how Leslie and Arthur would get to the bars. Leslie took great offense to the snub. Drunk yelling ensued.

Leslie and her friends traded insults across the room. None of their insults had the sting of Leslie's.

Leslie's insults were dipped in acid.

She told one friend, whose mother's nervous breakdown was town gossip, "Go to the crazy house with your mother, you ugly bitch."

She spit in another friend's face.

Arthur and Leslie stood on the front porch of her friend's apartment and waited for a cab.

The final seconds of the year ticked away.

Leslie covered her left fist with the sleeve of her jacket and knocked out her friend's living room window.

"Why are you doing that?" said Arthur, pulling her away from the glass. "Please, stop."

"Don't tell me what the fuck to do," said Leslie, ripping her arm free of Arthur's grasp.

"I hate you," said Arthur.

Leslie punched Arthur in the face.

They left for the city the next day.

TWO

The studio on Pulaski Street was a tiny cell of an apartment no more than three hundred square feet.

The apartment was not built to comfortably fit half a person, let alone Arthur and Leslie.

They left the apartment at every opportunity. They spent many nights in search of a fleeting, intangible purpose that one only finds at their most intoxicated.

They almost always conducted that search at their new favorite bar, Beloved.

Derek Blubbermann, who lived near Beloved and knew the owners, put Arthur in touch with a cocaine dealer as soon as Arthur got to the city.

All of the music writers scattered around Brooklyn at that time singlehandedly kept certain Colombian cartels out of the red. Cocaine was their fuel, and the private bathrooms at Beloved were perfect for snorting it.

Upon exiting Beloved's bathrooms, one was exposed to a litany of uninhibited youth. Cocktails and craft beer flowed down the extended bar counter. Smokers posed at the backyard tables. The entrance swelled with the names that populated relevant bylines.

In Beloved, lost souls lived out dreams of invincibility in a space that, when full, made Arthur and Leslie's apartment seem spacious.

The bar's close quarters, and the neurological state of its inhabitants, encouraged confrontation. Arthur and Leslie teamed up and carried out acts of violence for little more than the thrill of it.

On three separate occasions, Arthur fought strange men who were rude to Leslie. Leslie threw beer in those same men's faces and ripped out their hair.

Arthur and Leslie turned that same toxicity on each other. The Pulaski Street apartment was a war zone.

Arthur spent his days freelancing from the apartment. On most mornings, before he drove Leslie to the *Lice* office, he snuck one of her cigarettes while she showered.

When Leslie's pack was full, Arthur's actions went unnoticed. When Leslie's pack was low, she kept count.

On the morning in question, Arthur had the audacity to smoke Leslie's last cigarette.

"Buy your own fucking pack," she said, checking the container after her shower.

"You're a selfish bitch," he said.

Leslie hit Arthur in the face and assaulted him for the second time in two months.

Arthur filled up a glass of water and threw it in Leslie's face.

She stood there soaking wet.

"If you ever do that again, I will say that you hit me," said Leslie, wiping the water away from her eyes. "And I will get away with it because I'm white."

"Say that again," said Arthur, discreetly grabbing his phone to record video of the statement.

"If you ever throw water on me again, I will say that you hit me," said Leslie, wringing out her hair. "And I will get away with it because I'm white."

"I recorded that," said Arthur, holding up his phone. "If you ever lie on me and try to smear my name, I'm letting everyone know that you're a racist white bitch."

"And who's going to believe you over the white girl?" said Leslie, walking out into the freezing streets.

Arthur moved on from such incidents with remarkable speed because he had cocaine.

He spent up to a thousand dollars a week on the drug and consumed it in nearly lethal quantities.

When others stopped and waited for the weekend, Arthur kept going. The malicious stimulant kept him detached from the dismal reality of his situation.

He completed two, three, sometimes four freelance articles a week, despite his addiction.

When Arthur was alone on Pulaski Street, the apartment seemed like all the room in the world. He wrote nonstop. He only took breaks for cigarettes and cocaine.

His demented process came with the positive feedback of increased recognition. He had returned to New York to make a name for himself and it worked.

Arthur had an enormous ego, but no one could knock the confidence out of his sails better than Leslie. She would find him in his boxers, with cocaine residue on the desk, and berate him for how he spent his day.

"You're disgusting," she would say. "Take a shower, Arthur. Brush your teeth."

"I don't have to go to an office every day like you," he would respond. "I'll get dressed when we go out."

"How much money did you spend on cocaine today, Arthur? You won't help me out with rent, but you can spend all your money on drugs."

"Why should I have to help you with rent?"

"Because you're my boyfriend."

"Leslie, we barely even have sex."

"Here we go again. I need a bottle of wine."

11

"Relax, okay? I'm tired of carrying you home."

"Then give me some coke."

"I'm out."

"Then order some more. Where are we going?"

For all of their dysfunction, Arthur and Leslie were the life of the party.

Eyes lit up when they entered Beloved.

Their presence was electric because it guaranteed absurdity. Leslie's perpetual drunkenness lent itself to an unpredictable excitement. Arthur always had drugs.

Their relationship was bred on the type of chaos that is attractive from a distance.

Arthur and Leslie's sex was a pentagram shy of satanic ritual. They had sex after fights, once they exhausted verbal attacks and needed to release the remaining energy.

Sex was how Arthur and Leslie convinced themselves that they had a reason to stay together.

"Why don't we do this more often?" Leslie would ask, when it was over, catching her breath.

"I've been asking you the same thing for months," Arthur would say, putting on his T-shirt.

Outside of those moments, Leslie's attraction to Arthur dwindled, and it had ever since he attempted suicide in the apartment they now shared.

He came on to her often. She routinely denied his advances. Arthur sought reassurance elsewhere.

In those days, all it took was a unique voice and witty tweets to attract admirers on the Internet.

Arthur had his fair share, a truth that gave him delight in the face of Leslie's terminal indifference.

None had his heart more than Patty Olsen, a sex blogger and prominent feminist from New Zealand.

Patty had explicit conversations with Arthur daily. She gave him hope that his tormented existence with Leslie would expire.

"I can't wait to meet you," Patty would say, in direct messages. "We should run away. Leave everyone behind. Live off the land. Start a new life."

"I'd leave tomorrow," Arthur would type back. "I wish you were in bed with me right now."

"I just feel bad because I like Leslie. It's so complicated. I wish she treated you better."

"Me too."

"If anyone finds out about this, it will be bad for my reputation. I'm supposed to be supporting other women, not trying to fuck their boyfriends."

"No one's going to find out."

"Make sure you delete everything. Please."

"I will."

"You promise?"

"I promise."

Arthur kept his word. He deleted the messages. He deleted the nude photographs after he masturbated to them in the bathroom.

Patty booked a flight to visit her Internet friends in New York that spring.

She made plans with most of the people on the scene, including Leslie. The two of them arranged to get drinks with their mutual friend, Lace Logan.

On Patty's first night in New York, she went to Lace Logan's apartment.

Lace was a stunning Australian expatriate who did marketing work in the city. She was Patty's closest friend online, mostly because of shared interests, but also because they came from the same part of the world.

Arthur lusted after Lace with an unspoken intensity, but their relationship remained platonic.

Leslie was at Lace's apartment when Patty showed up, baggage in hand.

The three of them drank wine, took selfies, gossiped, and smoked.

Leslie texted Arthur.

"Patty's here," she said. "Come over to Lace's. She wants to meet you."

When Arthur arrived, he and Patty exchanged shameful looks.

A few days later, they met alone in her room at the Tribeca Blu on Canal Street.

Arthur thought that he and Patty would have sex. He moved his hand inside of her waistband a minute into making out. She stopped him.

"We shouldn't do this," said Patty, pushing away Arthur's hand. "I can't. I'm sorry."

"Is it because of Leslie?" asked Arthur.

"Yes," she said. "I wish we could, but it's different now that I've met her."

They laid in bed for another hour. They kissed a few more times. They knew it was the last time that their affair would be so physical.

Arthur had slept with men since high school but had not hooked up with a man who he considered a friend in years.

He pined for a few of his male acquaintances. He hoped they would surrender to the curiosities of same-sex experimentation, but that never happened.

Then Arthur became friends with Levi Borowitz.

Levi was a handsome Jewish boy two years older than Arthur. He was a Beloved regular and a senior editor at *Traction* magazine.

Arthur found Levi attractive from the moment they met. He had fantasized about him in the past.

One night at Beloved, Leslie got too drunk to stay. She and Arthur were fighting. Leslie got into a cab alone.

Arthur went back to Levi's apartment on Grand Street to finish the night's cocaine and order more.

Levi's boyfriend had just moved to Los Angeles to take a writing job on a popular television series.

"I'm worried that he'll get famous without me," said Levi, chopping lines on the glass dining table.

"That's what Leslie says when I tell her that we should break up," said Arthur, rolling a twenty-dollar bill into a tight, crisp cylinder.

Arthur and Levi had the lingering eye contact of which all illicit sex affairs are made. Arthur told Levi that he had been with men in the past.

Levi blushed.

"If you want to do something like that again," Levi said, holding eye contact, "I'm here."

Arthur's pulse rose.

Levi opened a bottle of whiskey. He grabbed two tumblers from the cabinet and poured a shot in each.

"I'm glad we're friends now," said Levi, raising his glass, exposing his lower stomach.

Levi wanted to show Arthur his vinyl collection. They walked over to the record player. Getting a record turned into making out and then they were in Levi's bed.

Arthur got a call from Nicky Ivanov about a work opportunity in Philadelphia.

Nicky was a Russian video director who Arthur had lived with in Harlem. Nicky knew a rapper who wanted to film a live interview with a journalist at his mixtape release party. Arthur would be paid.

Arthur drove down Interstate Ninety-Five and did what he had to do at the event. He got his money and a bag of MDMA and went to get water at the bar.

Arthur took the drugs out of his pocket when a beautiful, mysterious woman with a tempting smile walked up to Arthur and asked his deal.

"Who are you?" she said. "What are you doing?"

"I'm about to take this molly," said Arthur.

"I'm Josie," she said.

"Arthur," he said, pouring the MDMA crystals into the water. "Do you want some?"

Josie took a sip of Arthur's molly water. Arthur chugged the rest of the glass. They discovered that Josie's friend Vera Vine was friends with Nicky.

Arthur was under Josie's spell. He wanted to marry her that night.

Josie Akers was a nanny for a rich family in Harrison, New York. Josie was tall, a foot taller than Leslie. With heels, she was face-level with Arthur.

"Are you coming with us?" she asked Arthur.

Vera, Josie, Arthur, and Nicky went to Vera's apartment on the north side of Philadelphia. Josie rolled three joints. The four of them drank champagne.

Nicky and Vera went to Vera's bedroom and left Arthur and Josie downstairs alone.

"Tonight was fun," said Arthur.

"I agree," said Josie, flicking the lighter. "I'm going to be so tired when I see my boyfriend."

She took a hit and passed the joint to Arthur.

"Will this be the last time I see you?" said Arthur.

"It doesn't have to be," said Josie.

They exchanged numbers.

Leslie was restless at *Lice*. Summer was approaching and they had yet to give her a full-time position.

A new position was available at *Abstract*.

Leslie had left *Abstract* on shaky terms, but she worked hard to repair her relationships with editors there.

Leslie interviewed with *Abstract* and won over the staff a second time. She got the associate editor title, and they increased her salary by ten thousand dollars.

Arthur was not looking for a job, but he got an unexpected call from Pharaoh Woodson, legendary musician from production duo The Saturns.

"Arthur, I've been watching you," said the famous producer. "Your writing is powerful. I want you to meet a friend of mine. Are you available tomorrow?"

Pharaoh wanted Arthur to meet with Shawn Sapp, chief executive of the advertising agency Transition.

Arthur marched into Shawn Sapp's office and told him exactly how much money it would take for him to give up his freedom as a freelancer.

Shawn gave Arthur a six-figure salary on the spot.

The lease on Pulaski Street was about to end.

Arthur and Leslie wanted to give the relationship a chance in a better apartment. Maybe with more space, they would not get sick of each other so easily.

"I want hardwood, stainless steel, and a balcony with views," Leslie told Arthur.

Arthur found an apartment on Spencer Street. They went to look at it after work on a hazy June evening.

The place was huge and hit every item on their checklist. It even had a personal elevator.

"You found my dream apartment," said Leslie.

The next week, Arthur and Leslie each wrote a check for thirty-six hundred dollars to cover first and last month's rent and a security deposit.

In late June, Leslie had a birthday party at Beloved.

The week before Leslie's birthday, Arthur told Leslie to never let him do cocaine again and to stop him if she ever saw him trying to order it.

The fact that Arthur was coked out at Leslie's party was obvious to anyone with common sense.

Arthur and Leslie barely spoke to each other at the party, but Nicky Ivanov had driven to the party from Philadelphia and saw Arthur in his wrecked state. He mentioned Arthur's overconsumption to Leslie.

"I'm worried about Arthur," said Nicky. "He's gone too far with the blow. He's sweating. He's shaking. He looks like he might die."

Leslie bolted to the other side of the bar and pushed Arthur in the chest.

"Did you do cocaine tonight?"

"No."

Leslie slapped Arthur across his face so hard that the editor-in-chief of *Voyeur*, Jenna Carson, turned to look.

"You drug addict liar. You can't even stop doing cocaine for one night. *One night*. My birthday."

Leslie stormed out of the bar.

Levi walked over to Arthur and put his hand on Arthur's shoulder. "What was that?" he asked.

"Did you see the way she hit me in front of everyone?" said Arthur.

"She can hardly stand right now she's so drunk," said Levi. "Don't worry about it."

Leslie went home alone.

Arthur went home with Levi.

Independence Day was the weekend before Arthur and Leslie moved to the apartment on Spencer Street.

Leslie went home to Buffalo to spend the holiday with her family. Arthur stayed in the city.

The only person he knew who was still in the city was Lace Logan.

Arthur went to Lace's apartment. The drugs were already out. She poured him a glass of prosecco. They discussed plans for the night.

Lace's phone was stolen out of her purse while she and Arthur were on the dance floor at Kinfolk.

Arthur drove Lace back to her apartment. They tried to locate the phone with a GPS app. The phone was dead, or the person who stole it had turned it off.

They laid on Lace's bed and opened another bottle of prosecco. She spoke of how much she missed her family in Australia. She sent her father an email about the stolen phone. Arthur wondered if the stolen phone was his fault, if he brought bad luck to people's lives.

"Is there any way I can help?" said Arthur.

"Got any white left?" Lace asked. "I'm out."

Arthur dumped his cocaine on Lace's dresser. They snorted lines in between sips of prosecco.

Arthur tried to kiss Lace. She turned her head.

"Not happening," she said. "Maybe if you weren't with Leslie, but she's my friend."

"I'm not just trying to fuck," said Arthur. "I really care about you."

"I can't help you with that," said Lace, walking Arthur out. "You need to work on your relationship."

THREE

The condo on Spencer Street was a sprawling fortress of an apartment. Five of the Pulaski Street apartments could fit into the space on Spencer Street.

The apartment had hardwood floors, floor-to-ceiling windows, stainless steel appliances, a washer and a dryer, walk-in closets, and a balcony with a majestic view of Manhattan.

Arthur and Leslie were already popular because of the energy they brought to a room. Once they were able to provide the room itself, the sycophancy tripled.

As soon as Friday night struck, the same music writers that crowded Beloved could be found at Arthur and Leslie's apartment. Avalanches of cocaine gave their granite countertop a permanent off-white tint.

If only their relationship was as much of a success as their parties.

Arthur and Leslie fought about everything. No apartment, no parties, no career trajectory, and no satanic sex could stop the warpath that they were on.

The apartment became another carnival attraction in the mess that was their lives.

The tragedy of Arthur Simon and Leslie Nostril was inevitable. Their fate was sealed the moment they walked through the doors on Spencer Street.

The revelry only stalled the collapse for a moment.

But the collapse was coming.

Arthur's ego brought it on faster than it may have occurred under different circumstances.

He branched outside of music journalism and wrote an article about interracial dating for the culture blog *Voyeur*. He cited his relationship with Leslie as inspiration.

The article was a hastily written, imprudent effort, one that Arthur grew to regret, but it was successful in attracting the attention he craved.

Arthur's only goal was to create controversy, sometimes at the expense of his dignity.

Within a week, two million people read Arthur's article. Some thought the piece was powerful. Others thought it was an embarrassment.

Arthur received thank you letters and death threats. People loved him and hated him, but, more than anything, people knew him.

All Arthur wanted was to be known.

By the end of Arthur's first month on Spencer Street, book agents were knocking down his door.

After three months at Transition, he hit the wall that he hit at every job. No matter how high the salary, and no matter how easy the work, Arthur hated offices.

Once he could set his own schedule, nothing would get in the way of his drug habit.

Cocaine always won with Arthur.

He would show up to the Transition office with a pocket full of blow and sneak off to the bathroom to snort a few lines before he sat down at his desk.

When a literary agent called Arthur down to Union Square for a meeting, the change was welcome.

The agent told Arthur that the success of the *Voyeur* article made him a ripe candidate for a book deal.

Arthur's task was to write a book proposal. Then he would be rich.

The next day, Arthur quit his job at Transition.

He met up with Leslie in Times Square later that night and told her what happened.

"That's stupid," she said. "What about our rent?"

"I have money saved," said Arthur. "I need to focus on this proposal."

"You're not a good person," said Leslie. "You don't deserve a book deal."

Leslie wanted to drink.

"I'm going to see Derek," she said. "Are you coming to Beloved?"

"No," said Arthur. "I'm going to meet up with Ryan. I'll see you at home."

Arthur and Ryan met at Colador Cafe on Bedford Avenue.

They had not been friends for very long, but Ryan Irving was one of the few people who Arthur trusted.

Ryan was black like Arthur. He did not view Arthur as a threat or wish for his downfall.

Ryan lived half a block away from Arthur. They spent an exorbitant amount of time together during the summer of 2014, when Arthur most needed a friend.

Arthur constantly heard gossip about how other music writers hated him.

The gossip bothered Arthur because he was nice to his peers. He put them in touch with editors who gave them work, he listened to their problems, and he gave them advice. The music writers still despised him.

Arthur was too cocky. He spoke of his own successes too often. His behavior would have been better received if he was white, but he was not.

"I'm sick of these white boys," Ryan said, bluntly, over penne at Colador.

"I'm going to get the book deal and shit on all of them," said Arthur, biting into a panini.

Their drug dealer always took a long time. Arthur and Ryan always waited. A text message notified them of his imminent arrival.

"Tell me more about this book situation," said Ryan, chopping lines on the coffee table at his apartment.

"I want to go to Europe by myself and write the proposal," said Arthur, rolling a fifty-dollar bill. He leaned down to snort. "Leslie would kill me."

"Fuck that," said Ryan. "You have to go."

"I know," said Arthur. "I'll see what she thinks."

"No, don't ask her," said Ryan. He pulled up a travel website and handed his laptop to Arthur. "Do it right now. You have the money?"

Never one to fight an impulse, Arthur booked a one-way ticket to Paris for the following week.

Derek returned from the bar at Beloved with a glass of red wine for Leslie and a glass of whiskey for himself.

"How's your famous boyfriend?" Derek asked, mockingly, sipping from his glass.

"He's fine," said Leslie. "Someone wants to turn that *Voyeur* article into a book."

Derek slammed his drink on the table.

"I don't get it," he said. "Arthur is not famous. This scene is a bubble. He's a master marketer and manipulator, but he doesn't have real talent."

"I didn't know you had so many opinions about Arthur," said Leslie, finishing her wine. "Are you jealous?"

"No, he's an asshole," said Derek. "He thinks he's God's gift to Earth because he sends funny tweets every once in a while. I'm over it, and so is everyone else. Why are you dating him? Seriously."

"Things started out really well with us," Leslie said, getting defensive. She had her issues with Arthur, but it was difficult for her to hear others criticize him.

"That was two years ago," said Derek. "I used to like him too, but his head's gotten too big, and, most importantly, he doesn't treat you right."

"What makes you say that?" said Leslie.

"Come on. The day you two make it through a night at Beloved without getting into a fight is the day I think Arthur deserves a book deal."

Leslie had never looked at Derek romantically, despite how much Arthur suspected it, but that changed.

She wanted to be saved from Arthur, just as Arthur wanted to be saved from her.

"And how do you think I should be treated?" Leslie asked Derek.

She placed her hand on top of his and let it rest there for a moment.

Leslie did not feel like taking the subway or paying for a cab. She summoned Arthur to pick her up from Beloved.

The ride home was awkward.

Arthur did not tell Leslie that he had booked a flight to Paris. Leslie did not tell Arthur that Derek had joined the music writers who hated him, or that she had flirted with him after his admission.

It was difficult for Leslie to resist knocking Arthur down a few notches, but she loved the fact that someone appreciated her more than Arthur did. She wanted to keep that simple pleasure to herself.

They got home and rode the elevator up to their apartment on the eighth floor.

"I'm going to Paris next week," said Arthur.

The elevator chimed.

"Excuse me?" said Leslie. She walked into the apartment and set her purse down on the kitchen counter.

"I booked a flight," said Arthur. "I'm going to write the proposal there."

"You're kidding, right?"

"I'm not."

"Wait, so you quit your job, and you're taking a trip that you didn't tell me about nor invite me on?"

"That's one way of looking at it."

"When are you coming back?"

"It's a one-way ticket," said Arthur, bracing for the storm. "I don't know."

Leslie was hurt, but she masked her pain with rage. She ripped all of Arthur's clothes out of the closet. She pulled all of his books off the shelf.

"This is exactly why I'm getting as far away from you as possible," said Arthur.

"I hate you," said Leslie. "Take all of your shit and don't ever come back."

FOUR

Arthur landed at Charles de Gaulle. At baggage claim, he discovered that his watch was missing.

Arthur viewed the missing watch as debt he had to pay to the continent and motivation to replace it with the Rolex he was certain that he was soon to have.

The woman behind Arthur in the queue for cabs was a trombonist in the band for a famous musician's European tour. Arthur told her about his plan.

"It's better to fail at your vocation than succeed at someone else's," she said. "All the best writers did exactly what you're doing. You have to take that risk."

After Arthur booked the flight to Paris, he made plans to stay with a woman named Ruby, who he only knew from Twitter.

He hoped Ruby would fill the void that Leslie, Levi, Patty, and Lace had left in his life. He also thought Ruby would provide him with free housing in Paris.

On the cab ride into the city, Arthur got a direct message from Ruby that said she was sick.

A wave of guilt washed over Arthur.

He missed Leslie.

The last time Arthur was in Paris, he was with the ex-girlfriend from Chicago. That trip was the end of their relationship—Arthur met Leslie in the *Abstract* elevator the day he returned to New York—but it was better navigating foreign soil with someone else.

Alone in Paris, Arthur realized that he had not gotten away from himself.

Arthur bought French cigarettes. He went to Starbucks for Wi-Fi and American comfort. The barista spoke English, which made Arthur feel better.

He booked a room at Hotel Jardin de Villiers. The sun came out when he went outside to look for cabs. The beauty of Paris preserved his mental state.

He tried to hail a cab. The driver rolled up his window when he heard Arthur speaking English.

"We shouldn't have saved your ass in the war," said Arthur, as if he had personally stormed the beaches.

He took the Metro to his hotel.

The adventure was beginning.

Arthur loved the anonymity of being in another country. Even without Ruby, he thought that he should stay in Paris forever.

He dropped off his bags at the hotel and hit the streets with a notebook. He wrote in a restaurant across from the Panthéon. He wrote on a wooden bench across from the Arc de Triomphe.

He drank beer and smoked cigarettes and the words flowed like he knew they would.

Arthur did not work on the proposal, but he wrote down every moment of the trip as it happened. He thought that one day he could use the notes for a novel.

Arthur went to the Eiffel Tower.

He thought that he would find a woman to fall in love with under the Eiffel Tower.

He noticed a party taking place on the Seine.

Arthur did not have the wristband that permitted entrance. He talked his way in.

He saw several attractive women at the party. He could not work up the nerve to introduce himself. He drank alone and did not talk to anyone.

Arthur walked back to the Eiffel Tower and started to cut through the Champ de Mars when he saw a group of teenage boys passing around a bottle of gin.

He threw up his arms and yelled out to them.

"Where's the party at?"

"You tell us," one responded.

"I'm from New York," said Arthur. "I'm here writing a book, but I'm trying to have fun too."

"We're on gap year," a different one responded. "We just got here from Barcelona."

"I've always wanted to go to Spain," said Arthur, trying to nail down their accents.

"The girls are so fucking hot," said another.

"Where are you guys from?"

"Dresden, Germany," they replied, in near unison.

"The city that got bombed out?"

"That's the place."

The German boys handed Arthur the bottle of gin and told him that it was the end of their trip. They were in Paris for one more night. Then they were driving home.

"Are you staying in Paris?" one asked Arthur.

"No, I bought a one-way ticket," said Arthur. "I'm wondering if I should go to London, or go east to, like, Prague next. What do you recommend?"

"Prague is only a couple hours from Dresden, and it's beautiful," said the tallest one. "Come to Germany. We have extra space in our car."

Arthur left Paris with the Germans the next night.

After four hours of driving, they were on the Autobahn, tearing through the German countryside at two hundred kilometers per hour.

The Germans' names were Carl, Max, Lenard, and Phillip. All four of them were nineteen years old.

They told Arthur that most Europeans saw Americans as loud, arrogant, and overly patriotic.

"The weirdest thing for me, visiting New York City, was the American flags everywhere," said Carl. "Back home, if you show the least bit of patriotism, you're automatically a Nazi."

"Black Skinhead" came on shuffle and blasted through the car speakers. Arthur laughed at the irony.

They arrived in Dresden at noon.

The German boys dropped Arthur off in the city center and said their goodbyes.

Arthur took photos of the Frauenkirche and the Zwinger. He went to McDonald's for Wi-Fi and more American comfort. He needed reminders of home throughout his entire time in Europe.

A white man with red eyes tried to sell Arthur cocaine near the train station. Arthur felt like God was testing him and declined. He made a quiet promise to himself to detox from cocaine in Europe.

On the train to Prague, Arthur shared a car with a financial analyst from Philadelphia named Henry.

Henry worked at Morgan Stanley. He was also on a solo trek through Europe.

"That's so cool that you're a writer," said Henry. "I hate working in finance."

"I majored in accounting," said Arthur. "I know exactly what you mean. All the people I went to business school with are at accounting firms. I couldn't handle it."

Henry told Arthur about a bar crawl going on that night. He gave Arthur the name of the bar that the crawl started at and said to be there at 9:00 p.m.

Arthur checked into a room at Hotel Liberty that was the cheapest and largest of his trip. The room looked like something a communist dictator might have stayed in.

He dropped off his bags and immediately left the hotel to go see the Church of Our Lady Before Týn. The church had been the background on Arthur's computer for four years. He finally saw it in person.

Back at the hotel, he took a bath, put on a robe, and paced the massive room. He smoked cigarettes and drank whiskey while watching Czechoslovakian television.

Arthur did not make it to the bar by 9:00 p.m.

When he did get to the bar, he thought that Henry might be there waiting for him, but he was not. Arthur never saw or heard from Henry again.

The bar was crawling with tourists ready to party. Making friends was easy for Arthur in that environment.

A new bar crawl started every thirty minutes. After warm-up beers, Arthur's group set off into the night.

There were people from England, Italy, Australia, Ireland, Greece, Austria, and America in Arthur's group. Half of them were either doing cocaine or talking about doing it. Arthur wanted to indulge. He resisted.

The crawl ended at a five-story nightclub next to Prague Castle. The nightclub had a floor that played American rap music, but it was too crowded. Arthur left.

He went across the street and bought a döner kebab. He realized he was next to Charles Bridge.

Arthur started across the bridge when he noticed another group of teenagers drinking. They were staring at him so he did what he had done with the German boys and struck up a conversation.

The teenagers were from Slovakia. Their names were Helen, Mike, and Michael.

Helen and Mike appeared to be dating, so Arthur mostly interacted with Michael. Arthur told Michael that that he had been on one of the bar crawls.

"That's a tourist trap," said Michael. "We'll show you the real Prague."

The Slovakians took Arthur to Harley's, a bar in a cellar on Dlouha Street.

Harley's walls were covered with American flags, Harley-Davidson memorabilia, and Jack Daniel's insignia.

The teenagers bought Arthur four shots and asked him questions about New York City. Arthur got so drunk that he started to crave cocaine. He wished he had not turned down the cocaine in Dresden or on the bar crawl.

He asked the teenagers where to get drugs.

"I don't know about cocaine," said Michael, "but I can find cannabis or ecstasy."

Michael took Arthur to U Bukanyra, a bar in a houseboat docked on the Vltava.

The men holding drugs were standing on the dock in front of the boat. When they realized that Michael was with an American, they tripled the prices.

Arthur took that as a sign to call it a night.

"Before you go," said Michael, "I want to get you something you can't get in America."

Michael took Arthur to a grocery store, walked to the produce aisle, and picked up a samosa.

"We have samosas in America," Arthur said, laughing. "That's Indian food."

"You can get samosas in America?" said Michael.

"You can get anything in America."

Arthur overheard loud, male American accents coming from the front of the store.

He rushed to the front of the store and asked the Americans where they were from.

They were both in the Marines. One man was from Ohio. The other man was from Utah. They were traveling Europe together while on leave.

The Marines were with two women who lived in Prague and seemed to get a kick out of showing around tourists. The women's names were Sunny and Teresa.

Sunny was an expatriate from New Zealand who taught grade school. Teresa was an illegal alien from New York who was in the Czech Republic two years past her visa's expiration and made a living selling coke and molly.

Jackpot.

Michael left and went back to his Slovakian friends. Arthur thanked him for his hospitality and left the grocery store with the Marines, Sunny, and Teresa.

They headed towards U Bukanyra.

"I just came from there," said Arthur.

"We terrorize that place every weekend," said Sunny. "Prague's best junkies."

They stopped at Park Lannova to get their drugs in order. The Marines pulled out an eight ball and shoveled cocaine into their noses with hotel room keys. Arthur wanted to join in. He maintained his composure and settled for a large bag of MDMA.

He ate the MDMA crystals on the spot.

"Be careful with that," said Teresa. "It's pure, and it will completely fuck you up."

The five of them went to U Bukanyra. The Marines left on the dock because their flight to Turkey was in two hours. Arthur went inside with Sunny and Teresa.

The inside of the boat was sketchy. A sampling of "Prague's best junkies" were scattered across the room, strung out, slumped over secondhand sofas.

Arthur had not rolled so hard since the night he met Josie Akers. It was one of those highs where all he could do was lay back and close his eyes.

Sunny was high too. She kissed Arthur.

The sun came up. The boat was reduced to a state of panic and disbelief.

Sunny took Arthur back to her apartment in what was once a bloc of communist housing. He asked her questions about the building that she could not answer.

They got into Sunny's bed and listened to music. Arthur went down on her. She returned the favor.

Arthur checked out of Hotel Liberty two hours late. He bought a ticket for a train from Prague to Berlin for later that night. He had not slept, so he ate the rest of his MDMA for energy. He spent the day writing in bars.

Arthur got to the train station an hour before his train was scheduled to depart.

He woke up on one of the station's benches at the exact minute that his train left. He changed his ticket to a train leaving first thing in the morning. He had a night to burn in Prague and nowhere to stay.

Arthur wandered the streets looking for a place that he could sit in until the morning.

He wanted to find a bar, or a twenty-four-hour cafe, but everything was closed. The streets were very cold.

He went to a strip club.

Arthur's plan was to drink beer and watch naked women for a few hours, but a cute Hungarian stripper approached Arthur, took his hand, and led him to a back room for a lap dance.

After two dances, Arthur went with her to the champagne room. He stayed in the champagne room for four hours. The strip club charged ten thousand koruna to his debit card every hour. The Hungarian woman got naked and unfastened Arthur's belt. After she finished, she told Arthur about her family back home in Budapest.

Arthur boarded the train to Berlin without a second to spare. He tried to sleep, but spent most of the ride staring at the countryside, wondering if it was necessary to spend forty thousand koruna on a blowjob.

Arthur wanted to see the Berlin Wall. He went to the Reichstag first because it was closer to the train station.

He needed to kill time before he could check into his room at Hotel Allegra. He left his baggage at the front desk and stumbled along the Spree, exhausted. He smoked so many cigarettes that his throat became sore. The nicotine was all that kept him awake.

Arthur called Leslie for the first time in four days.

She was with Derek, pre-gaming for a party that she was hosting on Spencer Street.

"I'm sorry about the way I acted when you left," said Leslie, uncorking a bottle of red wine. "Put yourself in my shoes. You understand why I snapped, right?"

"Yes, and I'm sorry for not telling you about the trip," said Arthur. "I just needed time alone to work and focus. You understand why I had to do this, right?"

"I don't, but it's fine," she said, pouring a glass while Derek switched channels on the television. "When are you coming back?"

"I'm not sure."

"Can you come home tomorrow?"

"Leslie, I'm in Europe. It's not that easy. But it won't be more than a few days."

"Arthur, it's almost been a week. I don't know what you're doing. I need you, okay? Just get here."

"I'm coming. I'm looking into flights right now."

Arthur intended to book a flight right then and there, but he did not know from where he would depart. He wanted to go to one more city.

He checked in to Hotel Allegra. He sat on the bed and weighed his options. Exhaustion overtook his body as soon as he touched the mattress.

Arthur woke up six hours later.

He still wanted to see the Berlin Wall.

The walk from his hotel to the Wall took thirty minutes. He drank two beers on the way.

He spent the rest of the night at the Wall, chain-smoking, reading each placard, touching history.

Arthur considered heading east to Warsaw, but he had a craving for high-quality weed and did not feel like sniffing it out around Berlin.

In the morning, he bought a train ticket to Amsterdam and a flight that would leave from Amsterdam to New York City two days later.

The sky was dark when Arthur arrived in Amsterdam.

He went to a coffeeshop, bought an eighth of weed, and smoked joints at the bar for an hour.

Stoned, he ate two slices of cheese at New York Pizza that reminded him of home.

Arthur found a room at Bilderberg Hotel Jan Luyken. He could not check in until the next afternoon. The front desk held his baggage. He went out to explore.

De Wallen was his first destination.

Sex workers flanked by red neon lights stood in the windows of storefronts selling their bodies. Foreign men walked up to the glass and discussed prices.

Arthur locked eyes with a pretty Ukrainian woman who waved to him from her window. Fifty euros got him in the door. She rolled on a condom and put him in her mouth. She did everything else for a hundred euros more.

Arthur went to another coffeeshop. He met two Canadian men, Ian and Scotty, who were visiting from Vancouver. The coffeeshop sold psilocybin truffles. They bought a case of truffles and tripped together.

Amsterdam looked like an impressionist painting.

Albanian drug dealers in leather jackets offered Arthur cocaine, but he declined.

They went to Ian and Scotty's hotel room. The trip became too intense. Arthur vomited in the toilet.

He missed Leslie.

Arthur went outside to walk the streets by himself.

Two filmmakers from Atlanta recognized Arthur in the street and complimented him on his *Voyeur* article.

He met two men from Hoboken. He ditched them when they went to buy coke from the Albanians.

He met British boys from Chesterfield who were in town for a construction job. He sat with them in front of their hotel, drank beer, and smoked weed.

The sun came up.

Arthur said goodbye to the British boys. He walked along the canals looking for somewhere to eat.

He ate a Dutch pancake at a restaurant near the Anne Frank house. He tried to go to the Anne Frank house after breakfast. The line was too long.

Arthur had never seen so many people on bicycles in one place. He was almost hit by a cyclist when he crossed the street without looking.

Arthur stopped at Chanel on the way to his hotel and bought a fragrance for Leslie. The fragrance would be his peace offering when he set foot on American soil.

FIVE

Leslie was assigned her first cover story at *Abstract* when Arthur was overseas.

On the last weekend of September, she went to Los Angeles to interview her favorite artist, Vicki Menage.

Leslie returned to New York the first weekend of October. Writing the cover story was her top priority.

She offered to read Arthur the first draft. He was not interested.

Leslie opened a bottle of red wine and went to the balcony. She chain-smoked and worked on the story alone for six hours.

She came back inside and yelled at Arthur for wearing his shoes in the kitchen, on top of the freshly swept and mopped hardwood floor.

"You're psychotic," said Arthur. "You need help."

"I need help? Arthur, you're a cokehead and you don't have a job," said Leslie. "And that little book deal is never going to happen."

"When it does happen, I won't be dating you."

"Arthur, nobody likes you anymore. All of our friends thought that article was stupid."

"You think I don't know that all these crackers hate me? I don't give a fuck about our friends, Leslie. You can have all of them. I'm literally counting down the days until we move out of this apartment."

Leslie went to the bathroom, took a shower, shaved, brushed, flossed, applied makeup, sprayed on the Chanel, and told Arthur that she was leaving.

"I'm going to Beloved."

"Okay."

"That's it?"

"Yes, Leslie. I don't care."

"Look, I'm sorry about earlier. I just wanted you to help me with my story."

"I'll read it tomorrow."

"So you're not coming?"

"No. I'm waiting for acid, and I don't want to see Derek, or any of those people."

"I thought we talked about you doing drugs."

"It's not cocaine."

"If you want to take a shower and get ready now, I'll wait for you."

"I'm not coming, Leslie."

"God, I'm so sick of this."

Leslie got on the elevator. All that she could think about was her next glass of wine. No hope was left for she and Arthur. Time to self-destruct.

The acid kicked in just after midnight. The brick wall in the apartment melted into ominous figures and a thousand centipedes crawled across the floor.

The silver lining of the hallucinations was that Arthur would not have been able to handle the events of that night in any other state.

Arthur could not get a hold of Leslie.

His awareness of what was occurring manifested in the effects of the acid.

He looked at the Manhattan skyline and saw gigantic snakes scaling up the sides of the buildings.

Leslie texted Arthur at 3:53 a.m.

"I'm half asleep on Derek's couch. What's up?"

"Are you coming home?"

No response.

He sent another text. "Never mind. I know what you're doing, and it's okay."

Leslie came home at noon.

Arthur mimed sleep, but Leslie knew that he was awake. She sat down next to him on the bed and put her hand on his back. She was crying.

"I kissed Derek," said Leslie. "I slept in his bed in just my underwear. I think I love him."

"Okay," said Arthur, not moving. "That's fine. Me and you are obviously done."

Leslie cried more and said Arthur's name a dozen times. His face remained buried in the pillow.

"I know you fucked him," said Arthur. "You don't have to lie to me."

"We did not have sex," said Leslie.

"You gave him head. That's sex."

"I did not do that."

Arthur said, "I understand it, I accept it, I respect it," a hundred times in ten minutes. He rushed to the fifth stage of grief before he confronted the first.

Arthur lacked an initial emotional response because his heart was ripped out and he was numb.

Leslie stopped trying to break the wall of communication and left the apartment.

Arthur spent the day alone, in shock, compulsively smoking cigarettes to calm his nerves.

Leslie returned to the apartment and sat down next to Arthur on the bed. She was crying more than before.

"I met up with Derek to talk about last night," said Leslie. "We didn't have sex because he couldn't get hard. We were too drunk and coked out."

"Just tell me that you fucked him," said Arthur.

"I didn't. We did not have sex."

"What happened?"

"I touched him. He touched me."

Leslie tried to rub Arthur's back while he laid face down. He jumped up from the bed.

"Don't touch me."

Arthur ran to the couch and tried to sleep there. Leslie chased after him.

"Arthur, please, talk to me."

"Did you have sex with Derek?"

"No. I don't remember much, but I know that we did not have sex."

Arthur flipped over the coffee table. He threw a bottle of wine at the floor in an attempt to smash it and leave a mess. The bottle bounced up and dented the wall.

Arthur packed a bag and left the apartment.

Arthur was hardly home for the next three weeks.

He had sex with three new women to restore his ego, but he spent most of his time with Eleanor London.

Eleanor had moved from Oklahoma City to Brooklyn. Arthur crashed in her Park Slope apartment. They did so much coke and had so much sex that he occasionally forgot about Leslie.

On Eleanor's twenty-first birthday, in late October, she and Arthur went to Manny Rollins's apartment on Manhattan Avenue. Manny was Ryan Irving's friend from Boston. Ryan was at the apartment.

Arthur and Eleanor drove past Beloved.

"I hate being near that place," said Arthur.

"Why?" asked Eleanor.

"Because the guy who Leslie cheated on me with hangs out there and if I see him I'm going to do something stupid like jump out of the car and fight him."

Arthur parked in front of Manny's apartment and called Ryan. Arthur wanted to bum a cigarette, but he decided to prank Ryan first.

"It happened," said Arthur.

"What happened?" said Ryan.

"I saw Derek in front of Beloved. I jumped out of the car and fucked him up."

"Are you good?"

"No. The cops came. I'm coming to Manny's."

"You're with Eleanor?"

"Yes."

"Get over here. You're with a white woman and you just hit a white man."

"I'm kidding. Come downstairs. Bring me a cig."

Ryan laughed. "Wow. You really got me."

"The visions I had when I drove past there made it seem like it really happened."

Eleanor had MDMA that she wanted to take for her birthday. She and Arthur made glasses of molly water in Manny's apartment. The roll set in quickly.

Arthur, Eleanor, Ryan, and Manny left for Enid's. They wanted to get there in time to celebrate Eleanor's birthday at midnight.

Arthur tried to hail a cab.

"We don't need to take a cab to Enid's," said Manny. "It's three blocks away."

"I don't want to walk past Beloved," said Arthur. "I'll feel compelled to go in there."

"No, you won't," said Ryan. "You'll be with us."

An external force took over Arthur's body when they walked past Beloved. He ran inside before Eleanor, Ryan, or Manny could stop him.

Arthur scanned the room, looking for Derek.

Derek was at a table in the middle of the bar, laughing with four of his friends.

Arthur snuck up to Derek's table.

Derek did not notice Arthur until it was too late.

Arthur punched Derek's face as hard as he could.

Arthur returned to the apartment on Spencer Street at the end of October.

Leslie threw her arms around Arthur when he walked out of the elevator.

"I missed you so much," she said.

"I missed you too," he said.

That night was almost like old times.

Leslie was working on a large bottle of red wine. She invited Arthur to help her finish it. They got drunk and made out on the couch. Arthur ordered MDMA.

The drugs led to terrific sex, "maybe we should get back together" sex. Arthur and Leslie sprawled across the mattress, limbs interlocked.

"Why can't we be the couple who was strong enough to make it through a tough spot?" Leslie asked, sitting up in bed. "How do we make it work?"

"I need to feel like you're being honest with me about what happened," said Arthur.

"I am being honest. I have been this whole time."

"Did you have sex with him?"

"No. I swear. I did not have sex with Derek. I would not lie about that."

"Did you give him head?"

Leslie paused. "Yes. For a few seconds."

Arthur had a nervous breakdown in the morning. He kept silent and bottled the emotions until he could not.

"What's wrong with you?" Leslie asked.

"Nothing," said Arthur.

"Arthur, I can tell when you're upset."

"I'm not upset."

"Why have you been avoiding me all morning?"

"Because you sucked Derek's dick and you're a whore. There. You happy?"

"This is why I didn't tell you what happened."

"I'm going to ask you one more time. Please tell me the truth. Did you have sex with him?"

"No, Arthur. Nothing you do will get me to say that I had sex with Derek because I didn't."

Arthur picked up a flowerpot and smashed it on the ground. Black specks of dirt shot across the floor.

"You're sick, Arthur," Leslie said, fighting tears.

"No, you're sick for sucking some fat white boy's dick behind my back, you fucking whore."

"Fuck you, Arthur. I should have let you kill yourself in my kitchen."

"When I kill myself today, you'll get your wish."

Leslie left for work.

Arthur grabbed the sharpest knife in the kitchen drawer. He slashed his left wrist like he did the year before.

Arthur left a bloody rag on the granite countertop for Leslie to see when she got home.

He went to the bathroom, tied a belt around his neck, and tried to hang himself from the shower rod, but the shower rod collapsed into the bath.

Arthur needed drugs and sex.

He called Eleanor and told her to come over.

She stepped over the broken flowerpot and walked to the bedroom. They smoked two joints and tried to have sex. Arthur's mind was so clouded with hate that he could not perform.

Eleanor left.

Arthur booked a flight to Los Angeles. He ignored Leslie's calls all day. He flew out later that night.

Vanessa Johnson picked up Arthur from the airport. She was the Sounds by Surgeon Tre co-worker who Arthur had slept with when he lived in Los Angeles. Arthur crashed at her West Hollywood apartment. They did not have sex again because Arthur's libido was nonexistent.

Arthur spent his first two days in Los Angeles at the beach. He stared at the waves for long stretches of time. The distance from New York calmed him.

Derek wrote Arthur an email apologizing for what happened with Leslie. He said that he was too drunk that night. He said that he understood why Arthur hit him.

Arthur called Derek.

"Did you have sex with Leslie?"

"It's difficult to say," said Derek. "I'm sorry. We were both wasted. I don't remember."

Arthur called Leslie.

"Did you have sex with Derek?"

"No," said Leslie. "He couldn't get hard."

"That means you tried. I know how that goes. Was he inside of you at all for any amount of time?"

"We were naked and grinding."

"Did he ever go inside of you?"

"No."

"Leslie, tell me the truth. I'm begging you."

"He was inside of me for maybe ten seconds. I'm sorry. I was wasted. I can't remember."

Arthur keeled over with sickness in front of Vanessa's apartment on Fountain Avenue.

"I fucked three girls in Europe," said Arthur. "I fucked two girls from Twitter that I never told you about. I fucked Levi. I almost fucked Patty Olsen. I tried to fuck Lace. And I met someone in Philadelphia."

Leslie's jaw dropped.

"I knew it," she said. "I knew you were fucking cheating on me."

"We're even now."

"How can you be mad about Derek and ask me all of these gross questions when you've been with, I can't even count how many, other people?"

"You could have fucked anyone and I would have understood and been cool about it. But you chose someone who hates me, who I know."

"It's worse that I don't know who these girls in Europe are. Or the one in Philadelphia. I was honest with you. I came home and told you what happened."

"You told me part of what happened. You lied."

"Arthur, you've been lying our entire relationship.

"Leslie, it doesn't matter. I'll never get over what you did. It's hypocritical and selfish, but it's true."

"That's not fair."

"I didn't say it was fair. I fucked up too. But I can't be fake and pretend like I don't think about Derek's dick every time I look at your face."

"I was blacked out. I made a mistake. Someone who I thought was my friend took advantage of me. I'm not saying he raped me, but I was vulnerable, and I don't remember anything. I'm sorry. I understand why you cheated. I can forgive you. Can you forgive me?"

"I can't."

"Look, Arthur, I know how you feel. I'm going through the same thing. But I know we can make it through this. Years from now, we'll laugh about this. We'll laugh at everyone who doubted us."

Arthur went with Vanessa to the Sounds by Surgeon Tre office the next day.

He sat in on a meeting about an upcoming campaign and made several salient points. Arthur's former co-workers asked him to rejoin the company. They said he could work out of their new office in New York.

Arthur returned to New York and continued to live with Leslie in the apartment on Spencer Street.

Their peculiar living situation assumed a normalcy that briefly allowed them to operate as sane persons.

One night in late November, Leslie made spaghetti, bruschetta, and baked chicken for two of Arthur's friends who were visiting the city.

Arthur's friends were a male model and a female model from Toronto. They were dating each other and had gone for drinks with Arthur and Leslie earlier that day.

Arthur invited Ryan to dinner.

Leslie did not like Ryan.

She finished a glass of red wine and tore into him.

"Ryan, you look like a fucking homeless person with that beard," she said. "I didn't make dinner for you."

"Leslie, what's the problem?" said Arthur.

"I don't even know who these fake ass models are either. Everyone needs to leave right now."

"Why don't you go suck Derek's dick," Arthur said, in front of the company.

Leslie smacked Arthur in the face, on the couch.

"Fucking bitch," said Arthur, standing up.

Leslie jumped to her feet and tried to smack Arthur again, but he blocked her. The kinetic energy of her blow being stopped sent her to the ground.

Ryan threw his plate of spaghetti into the sink and grabbed his backpack.

"We need to go," said Ryan, motioning to the models. "Arthur, you should leave too. If you need anyone to corroborate what happened here, I got you."

Ryan and the Canadians got on the elevator and left. All three of their faces were tense from what they saw.

Arthur and Leslie were left alone in the apartment.

"I'm calling the police and having you arrested," said Leslie. She sat on the couch and opened her phone.

"You hit me," said Arthur. "I should call the police and have you arrested."

"Yeah? And who are they going to believe between the two of us?"

"We have three witnesses. And I still have that video from last year. Try me."

"You're a piece of shit and I hope you die. I hope the next time you do a line your heart explodes. This is why I went and cheated on you with white dick."

Arthur picked up Leslie's half-empty glass of wine off the countertop and threw the wine in her face.

Her clothes and the couch were stained.

Arthur wanted to leave the apartment and walked towards the elevator when Leslie threw the wine glass at the back of Arthur's head. The glass missed his head and shattered into a dozen fragments on the floor.

The elevator opened.

Arthur got on the elevator. Leslie chased after Arthur and pulled him back into the apartment.

Arthur ripped his arm free from Leslie. He pressed the button on the wall to call the elevator again.

Leslie dropped to the ground and cried. She begged Arthur to stay.

"I'm sorry, Arthur. There's too much going on. Please stay here with me. I hate it when you leave."

She accidentally stuck her hand in a shard from the broken wine glass on the floor. The cut spread across her left palm. She screamed. Blood dripped from her hand.

Arthur carried Leslie to the bathroom.

He helped clean her bleeding hand while she stood in the shower sobbing. He left the bathroom. He swept up the broken glass. He mopped up the blood.

Leslie got out of the shower and wrapped a blue washcloth around her hand. She and Arthur went to bed. They kissed and held each other tightly.

"Thank you," said Leslie. "It's not your fault. I'm so fucking drunk and stupid and I cut my hand."

"Don't thank me," said Arthur. "I want to help you. But this is why we can't be together. It's dangerous."

Leslie went to urgent care in the morning.

The cut on Leslie's hand required six stitches.

SIX

Arthur and Leslie changed after that shard of glass sliced open Leslie's palm. They talked more. They fought less. The stitches had a strange way of calming them.

Arthur had not seen Derek in person since punching him. He built up Derek's image in his mind. Arthur wanted to see Derek again, to witness his putridness in the flesh. To delete the image.

One night in mid-December, Manny Rollins hosted a party at his apartment on Manhattan Avenue. Ryan Irving invited Arthur but warned: "Derek is here." Arthur joked that if he came over he would punch Derek again, but, in his heart, he wanted closure.

Arthur left Leslie on Spencer Street. His car flew down Bedford Avenue blasting Eminem.

Arthur spent his first hour at the party being loud, snorting coke, and flirting with every girl in the room. He wanted Derek to notice him and see how happy he was and fear getting hit again.

His behavior was a facade.

Underneath, in the repressed chamber, Arthur felt small, childish, and inadequate.

He walked up to Derek.

"I'm over it, okay?"

"I'm sorry, man."

"I know. But I'm not tripping off that shit anymore. We did what we did. We're young, wild savages. My life is great. I'm over it."

"It's still not cool. I fucked up. I feel terrible."

"You know how many dudes' girlfriends I've fucked out of spite? It was karma. I'm fine with it."

Arthur studied Derek closely. He wondered what Derek looked like naked. He obsessed over nailing down exactly what Leslie experienced that night. He wanted to have a threesome with Derek and Leslie.

Arthur did not get his threesome, but he executed another objective.

Derek had been DJ'ing at Beloved. He played to small groups of friends every other weekend.

Arthur wanted to throw a party at Beloved.

Arthur did not know how to DJ, but he did not care. He thought serious DJs were pretentious. He thought that if an aux cord and a laptop was all one needed to play music, that he should play music.

Such blatant disregard for the craft seemed punk to Arthur. He thought it democratized the field. He thought it proved that the best nights were based solely on energy, not technique. The only technique that mattered was playing songs in the correct order.

(Aux cord DJing, as it became known, was relevant for eleven months. It has since died off and is regarded as a joke of mid-2010s ephemera.)

Arthur and Derek agreed to throw a party together. It would be held on the last Friday in January.

The line in front of Beloved stretched so far down Manhattan Avenue that Arthur thought he was famous.

He showed up in a black, tinted SUV, wearing fake fur and eight hundred dollar pants.

The turnout for Arthur's party was the surge of self-esteem that he needed. There was never a line in front of Beloved when Derek DJ'd alone.

Arthur stood on the steps of Beloved in his obnoxious fur coat. He fielded the yells and screams from people trying to get into a bar that, in its existence, had never dealt with such a large crowd.

Arthur saw Maggie Harvey. He grabbed her hand and brought her inside as others stared and groaned.

What impressed Arthur more than seeing the usual cast of music writers, some who he knew disliked him, were the nameless faces of people he did not know.

Arthur had fans.

The editor-in-chief of *Voyeur*, Jenna Carson, bought Arthur a beer.

"I hear they're turning your article into a book."

"I still have to write the proposal, but yes, there's an opportunity."

"That's going to be a bestseller. People love you."

"You think?"

"Arthur, when I was outside trying to get in an hour ago, people were chanting your name. I don't know what you're doing right now, but it's special. We should celebrate. Let's do some lines."

Derek won the battle. Arthur won the war—if one considers cheap, Brooklyn-centric fame a victory.

The music writers buzzed with rumors that the rapper Rake was releasing a new mixtape in February.

Arthur wrote many articles about Rake and he was a devoted fan of his music.

Most people were Rake fans back then. He had platinum albums, number-one singles, and the same worldwide renown Arthur wanted for himself.

Rake followed Arthur on Twitter on Christmas. They had direct messaged three times by February.

One night in mid-February, Kanye West hosted a free concert in Madison Square Park to celebrate the launch of his clothing line.

The Sounds by Surgeon Tre office was a block away from Madison Square Park. Arthur desperately wanted to attend the concert.

Leslie showed up to Arthur's office with an extra ticket. They walked to the park together. Weather forecasters said it was the coldest night in a hundred years.

After the concert, Arthur and Leslie noticed a mob of shrieking fans shouting at a celebrity surrounded by security and an entourage in matching blue jackets.

Arthur realized that it was Rake.

He hopped over a barricade and walked through the mob, towards Rake.

He was stopped by Rake's security. Rake saw the commotion and looked in Arthur's direction. Arthur shouted "Arthur Simon! I'm Arthur Simon."

Rake told security to clear a path for Arthur. Arthur walked into Rake's inner circle.

"Pleasure to meet you," said Arthur. "I'm a big fan of everything you do."

"The feeling is mutual," said Rake.

"Why did you follow me on Twitter?"

"You're making waves right now, man. Everybody reads those articles."

"Damn. That's an honor. Thank you.

"You're a wise guy, Arthur. I've been watching you for a while now."

"What are you about to do right now? You just shut down the whole block."

"That's nothing compared to the way you just pulled up on me," Rake said, laughing. "There's supposed to be some after-party for the concert. I don't know."

"Well, I'm about to head back to Brooklyn. How do we stay in touch?"

"I'll give you my number. Text me."

Rake gave Arthur his number.

Arthur and Rake took a picture together. Arthur strutted back to Leslie, who was too short to hop over the barricade as easily as he had.

"Don't forget who got you the tickets," said Leslie. "I made that possible."

"I know. Thank you, Leslie. Seriously."

"What did you guys talk about?"

"He just said that he liked my writing, and we took a picture together."

"Did you post it yet?"

"I'm about to."

Arthur and Leslie went for drinks at the Hog Pit around the corner.

When Arthur posted the photo with Rake, his phone got so many notifications that the battery died.

Arthur charged his phone and turned it back on.

Rake had posted a photo of himself with the caption: *Walk in like I'm Arthur Simon.*

Arthur got text messages and phone calls from people who he had not seen or spoken to in years.

"What are people saying?" Leslie asked, glancing over at Arthur's phone.

"It's hard to keep track," said Arthur. "There's too much going on. Everyone's texting and tweeting 'Walk in like I'm Arthur Simon' and asking what it means."

"Oh my God," said Leslie, intensely swiping at her phone's screen.

"What happened?"

"Rake dropped the mixtape."

Arthur and Leslie closed their tab and ran to Arthur's office so that Leslie could get on a computer and make sure *Abstract* was covering the surprise release.

They downloaded the mixtape. Leslie worked while Arthur danced around the office.

Arthur wanted to party. He wanted to snort cocaine. Leslie went home to sleep. Arthur met up with Ryan Irving, and their new friend, Aaron Riley, at Enid's.

Aaron was half-Jewish, half-Korean. He had a physics degree from the University of Chicago but, somehow, wound up meddling in the scene.

Enid's was closing. Arthur, Ryan, and Aaron were the only people in the bar. The bartender was playing Rake's new mixtape.

After Arthur snuck off to the bathroom with Ryan for a few bumps of cocaine, he approached the bartender.

"I've been to a lot of great parties here," said Arthur. "How do you pick DJs?"

"We like anybody who can bring a crowd," said the bartender. "Most of our nights are booked, but we switch up the rotation when we can."

"It seems like everyone in Brooklyn DJs now."

"It's good business. Last weekend, Beloved—you know, that bar up the street—had a line down the block because some, like, famous writer kid was throwing a party there. The owners are my boys. They were stoked."

"That was me, dude."

"What do you mean?"

"That was my party."

"Oh shit. Why don't you do one with us?"

"When can we get in here?"

"Well, this is short notice, but we have an opening on Sunday. Would that work?"

Monday was President's Day. Most people had the day off from work. Arthur knew that a Sunday night party would draw an impressive crowd.

Arthur, Ryan, and Aaron decided to call their party the Book Club.

Arthur looked out from the DJ booth and saw the floor of Enid's packed with music writers and anonymous fans from the Internet.

People moshed, took drugs, and stood on tables while Arthur, Ryan, and Aaron played music.

The Book Club tore Enid's apart on Sunday night, and they made the bar a lot of money. The owners asked them to throw another party the next month.

Arthur and Leslie drove to Manny's apartment one Friday after work. When they got out of the car, Leslie realized that she did not want to be there.

"Arthur, can you take me home? I don't want to do cocaine with your friends."

"Leslie, you told me to find something to do tonight. Come on. I leave for Los Angeles next week. We'll just make an appearance."

Leslie wanted Arthur to love her. She wanted him to care about how she felt as much as he cared about her night with Derek.

Wine always decimated whatever small filter Leslie had over the words that came out of her mouth.

After ten minutes of feeling alone and annoyed in the apartment, watching Arthur laugh with Manny, Ryan, and Aaron, Leslie grabbed Arthur's car keys off of the wooden kitchen table.

"I'm sick of this," she said. "Everyone here sucks. Arthur, if you don't drive me home, I'm taking your car."

"Leslie, you're drunk. I'll get you a cab."

Arthur tried to pull the keys out of Leslie's hand. She jerked her hand away from his.

"Give me the fucking keys, Leslie. I'm serious."

Leslie punched Arthur in the face harder than she ever had. Everyone in the apartment witnessed it.

"Fuck you, Arthur," Leslie yelled. "I bet none of your boys know you fucked Levi."

Manny escorted Leslie to the door.

"You can't yell like that in my apartment," said Manny. "The neighbors will call the cops on us."

"Good. They'll arrest you for all of this coke."

"Leslie, you need to leave."

"I got her," said Arthur, attempting to shepherd Leslie out of the apartment.

"Get your fucking hands off me," Leslie shouted.

Arthur followed Leslie downstairs to make sure she got into a cab.

Arthur hailed a cab. Leslie got inside, but she jumped back out before the cab pulled off.

Leslie ran up to Arthur's car and kicked the passenger side door with her black suede boots.

When Arthur tried to stop Leslie, she spit in his face and yelled "He's hitting me!" on the street.

A pedestrian woman stopped, saw that Arthur was not hitting Leslie, and continued walking.

Arthur went to Aaron's apartment on Lefferts Avenue at the end of the night.

They sat facing each other on Aaron's couch.

"Just so you know, I don't care about what Leslie said earlier," said Aaron.

"About what?" said Arthur.

"Levi or whatever."

"I don't care either. It's not a big secret."

"Just saying, I understand more than you realize."

"You've been with guys before?"

"A couple experiences. When I was younger."

Arthur made eye contact with Aaron.

"Do you want an experience like that again?"

Aaron paused and looked away.

"I do. But I don't think it's a good idea."

Aaron went to his bedroom.

Arthur slept on Aaron's couch until 4:00 p.m.

SEVEN

Los Angeles became Arthur's sanctuary.

He went to Los Angeles under the guise of working the Indio Festival for Sounds by Surgeon Tre. He really wanted to revisit the paradise he left for Leslie.

On Arthur's first night in town, he got a text from Rake: "Where you at? Come to my crib."

The guard at the entrance to Rake's gated neighborhood in Calabasas told Arthur that Rake had reached his limit on guests for the evening.

"I'm coming for you," Rake texted, when he heard that Arthur was having trouble getting in.

A black, tinted SUV arrived at the gate. The driver lowered his window and called out Arthur's name.

The SUV pulled into the driveway of Rake's sprawling estate. Arthur saw a basketball court, foreign cars, and women standing by a side door, waiting to check their phones with security.

A member of security escorted Arthur to the front of the line and into the house.

Arthur walked up a single flight of stairs to the kitchen. The lighting had a neon glow that made reds look orange and blues look purple.

Rake was posted against the kitchen counter, wearing a red sweat suit with gold owl embroidery.

Rake greeted Arthur like he had known him for a decade. It was a normal weekday night, but the spread on the counter resembled the catering at a billion-dollar company's holiday party.

Rake offered Arthur a drink. They walked to the bar in the next room. Bystanders were visibly thrilled when Rake passed them.

"Kanye would be here if he wasn't in Armenia," said Rake. "He just bought a house down the block."

Arthur and Rake went behind the bar. Arthur drank whiskey. Rake drank beer. Bottles of Dom Pérignon lined the shelves of the bar.

Arthur and Rake talked for twenty minutes. They talked about Rake's upcoming performance at Indio Festival. They talked about not calling their mothers often enough. Women lingered nearby and introduced themselves when they sensed a lull in the conversation.

The night ended shortly after Arthur stood on the grand piano in Rake's living room and sang one of Rake's songs to the crowd at the party.

Arthur had to be at the Sounds by Surgeon Tre office in Culver City in the morning.

He took a cab back to Vanessa's apartment and passed out on the couch.

The next morning, Arthur posted a photo of himself with Rake from the night before.

Leslie called Arthur when she saw the photo.

"You were at Rake's house last night?" she asked.

"Yes."

"How did that happen?"

"He asked me to come over and sent his address."

"I thought you were in Los Angeles for work."

"I am. I'm heading to the festival now."

Tommy Aldrich gave Arthur a ride to Indio. Tommy was a manager for two musicians performing at the festival. He let Arthur stay at the desert house he rented for his artists.

Arthur dropped off his bags, took an MDMA pill from one of Tommy's artists, and left for the festival.

Arthur ran into Levi Borowitz on the festival grounds. Arthur was rolling face by then. He tried to kiss Levi. He was rejected. Levi had gotten engaged to his boyfriend and wanted to remain faithful.

Arthur and Levi still flirted. Arthur laid his head in Levi's lap and stared into his eyes.

"I'm surprised you're not backstage," said Levi, running his hands over Arthur's shoulders. "You're big time now, hanging out with Rake and all."

"I guess. It's weird. One picture and all of a sudden everyone is on my dick."

Levi left to cover a performance for *Traction*.

Arthur went back to Tommy's house and smoked a joint in the hot tub with the artists.

Arthur woke up and ate a bag of mushrooms that were on the kitchen counter at Tommy's house.

He went to the festival and mooched weed from 50-year-old music industry executives in the artist lounge. He stared at psychedelic patterns in the grass.

Agonizing stomach pain reminded Arthur that he was poisoning himself for leisure. The pain passed. Arthur went to scope out the scene backstage.

He passed a woman in an ankle-length blue coat. She was wearing sunglasses and smoking a blunt.

Arthur made a sharp turn when he realized it was Brianna, the famous pop singer. Arthur tapped Brianna on the shoulder and said, "You're a goddess."

Brianna put out her blunt on the palm tree between them. She turned away without saying a word.

Tommy texted Arthur about a dinner Rake was hosting and sent the address. The line for cabs was long. The dinner would be over by the time Arthur got one.

He walked a mile up the road outside of the festival and waved down a pizza delivery guy driving out of a gated community. The delivery guy said he would drive Arthur to the restaurant Rake was at for extra money.

The restaurant was called the Nest. Black, tinted SUVS lined the entrance. Security remembered Arthur from the night at Rake's house and let him inside.

Rake was sitting at the main table and motioned for Arthur to come over. Arthur told Rake that he wanted to write about their time together.

"That's cool, but you have to do one thing: make sure you mention that I had chicken in my pasta, not Italian sausage," said Rake. Awkward silence. "I'm kidding. I just hope you like the show."

Arthur went outside and smoked two cigarettes. Rake took photos with the restaurant staff and went home to rest up for his performance.

Arthur took a cab to a mansion party that a famous designer was throwing three miles away.

Festival security did not let Arthur backstage for Rake's performance. Arthur tried to convince the hulking men that he knew Rake. He was unsuccessful.

Rake's security showed up to sweep the premises before the performance and shouted, "Arthur is good," at festival security. They cleared the way for Arthur to enter.

Celebrities stood backstage socializing, drinking top-shelf liquor, and smoking joints. Rake watched from the doorway of his trailer then disappeared back inside.

Rake's performance was not well-received by festivalgoers or people who watched the live stream online. Indio Festival was the first failure of Rake's career.

Music industry executives and fellow celebrities congratulated Rake at his after-party later that night. They sheltered him from the incoming criticism.

Rake walked up to Arthur.

"What did you think?" he said.

"It was good," said Arthur.

"Be honest with me, man."

"I can see how some found it underwhelming, but people hate everything."

"Nah, I took a loss," said Rake. "I have to reassess what went wrong with my judgment."

Arthur went back to Los Angeles. That time, he did have sex with Vanessa before he flew home to New York.

Vanessa sat at her kitchen table and worked on a marketing assignment for Sounds. Arthur sat across from her and worked on his Rake story.

Arthur went twenty hours without sleep. He wrote about every facet of his week with Rake. He wrote about the drugs, the performance, and the scene at Indio Festival in glorious detail. The story was more a manifestation of Arthur's crumbling mental state than a Rake story.

Arthur published "Rake in Real Life" on *Abstract*'s website the next day.

EIGHT

Arthur's story set off a firestorm of conversation among the music writers. The reception trumped that of his *Voyeur* article, many times over.

Twitter users compared him to great writers of the past. Criticism outlet *Record* published an editorial about Arthur's story and how it would affect first-person journalism in the future.

Rake texted Arthur: "Incredible piece. You're smart as fuck. I feel like you understand my position, and I'm proud to call you a friend."

The reigning criticism against Arthur's story was that he had been too sympathetic to Rake.

But four million people read the story.

Arthur's agent called Arthur after the *Record* editorial went live.

"Arthur, stop slacking on getting your proposal done. You're happening right now. It's time to sell."

Leslie found a new apartment and planned to move out of the Spencer Street apartment in June. Arthur and Leslie would live together for another five weeks.

"Where's the new apartment?" Arthur asked, after he returned from Los Angeles.

"A little bit deeper into Brooklyn," said Leslie, washing wine glasses from the day before.

"Who are you living with?"

"A guy from work. The timing was perfect."

"That's great," said Arthur. "I'm happy for you."

Leslie did not want Arthur to be happy for her.

Leslie wanted Arthur to grab her and tell her that he loved her and that she should not move out and that they could make the relationship work.

Arthur wanted to reconnect with Josie Akers.

Arthur and Josie had not spoken much since the night they met in Philadelphia. Over a year had passed since that night. Arthur heard from Nicky Ivanov, who heard from Vera Vine, that Josie was single.

"If you're ever down in the city, you should come to one of my parties," Arthur texted Josie.

"Me and my girls are already planning on coming to your party next week," Josie texted back.

Arthur was surprised to receive such an enthusiastic response.

"You just made the best decision of your life," he replied. "I'll see you next week."

The Book Club usurped Arthur's professional efforts. Arthur knew the Book Club was silly, but it was fun. He thought that throwing fun, successful parties without a traditional DJ was a postmodern commentary on the craft.

What began as a postmodern commentary on DJing, and parties themselves, had become a formidable force in Brooklyn nightlife.

The Book Club got too big for Enid's. Arthur, Ryan, and Aaron moved their party to Kinfolk.

The first Book Club party at Kinfolk was in late April. The success of Arthur's Rake story heightened his local fame significantly. The line in front of Kinfolk wrapped around the block.

Arthur saw Josie walk into Kinfolk. He locked eyes with her across the room.

Josie headed straight for Arthur. They exchanged brief pleasantries, raising their voices so that they could hear each other over the loud music.

"I've always loved you," said Arthur, caressing Josie's soft face.

"I love you too," said Josie, staring into Arthur's brown eyes and touching his wrists.

Arthur and Josie kissed for the first time right there in the DJ booth at Kinfolk.

Leslie was at Kinfolk too.

Leslie was with Eleanor London, who she was trying to mentor. Leslie felt sorry that a guiltless young woman had become entangled in she and Arthur's mess.

But there was spite and competitiveness at play in Leslie and Eleanor's relationship. They were only friendly on the surface. Underneath, they wanted to best the other woman. They both vied for Arthur's attention at the party.

Arthur and Josie kissed enough to suggest what might happen between them but remained coy about their budding romance. They made plans to meet up later and then they mingled on separate sides of the party.

That separation gave Arthur enough space to manage Leslie and Eleanor.

Arthur found Leslie sharing a cigarette with Eleanor outside.

"Did you two have fun?" asked Arthur.

"So much fun," said Eleanor, exhaling smoke. "I've never been to a party like that."

Leslie laughed. "It was fine. You should learn how to DJ if you're going to throw parties."

"Well, I'm glad you enjoyed yourselves," said Arthur. "I'm about to meet up with some friends."

"No, Arthur," said Leslie, putting out the cigarette beneath her sneakers. "You're coming with me."

"Leslie, I made plans with other people."

"Made plans to do what? Spend the rest of the night doing cocaine?" Leslie grabbed Arthur's wrist and led him towards a cab waiting outside of Kinfolk. "That's not happening. Get in the cab."

Arthur did not want to make a scene. He opened the door and got into the cab. Leslie followed.

"Can I come?" said Eleanor, standing on the pavement, peering into the cab.

"Sure," said Leslie.

Leslie was apartment sitting for a co-worker who lived in Crown Heights. The three of them went there.

When they arrived at the apartment, Leslie grabbed Arthur's hand and led him to the bedroom, leaving Eleanor stranded on the couch in the living room.

They sat on the bed. Leslie was drunk.

"Arthur, I miss you."

"You don't have to miss me. I'm right here."

"But it's not the same."

"Things change, Leslie. That's good for us. I'm still here. I still got you."

"But you don't love me anymore."

"We've been through a lot together. I'll always respect you. I'll always appreciate you."

"Have sex with me one last time."

"Eleanor is in the other room. You're being super rude to her right now."

"Fuck Eleanor. Have sex with me."

Leslie tried to kiss Arthur. Arthur moved his face. Leslie jerked her head back in disbelief. She tugged at Arthur's bright pink hoodie.

"One last time, please."

"No, Leslie. No."

"One last time, then never again. I need closure. I need to know that you love me."

"Leslie, we're broken up. We can't do this."

Arthur put off Leslie's advances for another fifteen minutes. Late stage effects of the red wine Leslie drank at Kinfolk set in. She fell asleep on the bed.

Arthur went into the next room. Eleanor was on the couch, waiting, with a joint.

"What happened with Leslie?"

"She's drunk. She fell asleep."

Arthur sat next to Eleanor on the couch.

"Want to come back to my apartment?" she said.

"I have to get ready for work tomorrow," said Arthur. "You should go home."

Eleanor put her hand on Arthur's thigh. She moved her hand up and down his tight black jeans.

"We can stay here if that's easier."

"No, I'm about to leave. I'll pay for your cab."

They went outside.

Arthur opened the cab door for Eleanor and gave the driver cash. She stared at him through the rear window as the cab drove off into Crown Heights.

Arthur's cab showed up two minutes later.

Vera Vine had recently moved to Brooklyn. Josie was staying at Vera's apartment in Bushwick for the weekend.

Arthur was in a rush, backseat driving his cab, because it was past 4:00 a.m. and he could not believe that Josie was staying up so late for him.

"You up?" Arthur texted.

"Yes, where are you?" Josie texted back.

"In a cab. On my way. Linden Street, right?"

Arthur heard the music blasting outside when his cab pulled up to Vera's apartment on Linden Street.

He heard Josie and Vera singing Rake songs as he climbed the stairs to the third floor.

Josie opened the door to the apartment. "You made it. Now join us," she said, blushing.

Josie took Arthur's hand and led him to the living room. She was wearing tight black pants and a tight black midriff top. Arthur's pulse rose when he saw her exposed back and lower stomach.

Arthur, Josie, and Vera passed around a bottle of white wine and multiple joints.

Arthur and Josie danced closer than they had at Kinfolk. Vera went to bed and left them alone.

When Arthur and Josie kissed, a true euphoria consumed his body. The feeling did not have the artifice of a drug-induced high.

Vera's roommate was gone for the weekend. Arthur and Josie went to the roommate's bed. They kissed for another hour. They kissed with the intensity of two people who have not ruined each other.

Arthur ran his hands across Josie's back and lower stomach. Josie reached her hands under Arthur's bright pink hoodie and touched his chest.

Arthur removed Josie's tight black pants and went down on her. Josie did the same with Arthur's tight black jeans and went down on him.

They took off each other's shirts. Arthur got on top Josie. They pressed their bodies together.

Then she stopped him.

"We're not having sex," said Josie.

"That's cool. No pressure," said Arthur.

"I've only had one one-night stand. It was terrible and I hated it. I can't separate love and sex and I cried when it was over," said Josie.

Arthur was a hopeless romantic. He was already having visions of a future with Josie.

"This is not a one-night stand," said Arthur. "I love you. I know every guy says that, but I mean it. I love you, and I want to be with you forever."

"I love you too," said Josie.

Arthur and Josie's sex was divine. Angelic choruses of "oh my God" rang throughout the moonlit room. The experience left them breathless.

"When will I see you again?" asked Arthur, kissing Josie's neck on top of the wet, tousled bed sheets.

"I'm moving to Brooklyn tomorrow," said Josie.

"What? Are you serious?"

"Yes. Vera's roommate is moving out and I took the room. This is technically my room now."

"Wow. We're having a baby."

Josie laughed and pressed her lips against Arthur's once more before they fell asleep.

Arthur did not leave Josie's side for the next ten days.

He helped Josie move into the Linden Street apartment when she arrived with a car full of belongings from her apartment in Port Chester, a town neighboring Harrison, where she worked.

He went to the Spencer Street apartment and stuffed a backpack full of clothes so that he could crash with Josie and stay away from Leslie until she moved out.

Arthur and Josie acted as if they were married from the very beginning. They had both recently gotten out of abusive, stagnant relationships and took to the other with instant adoration and affection.

They stood on street corners and made out while the sky poured thick droplets of rain from above.

They took MDMA and watched *Clueless* while cuddling on the couch in Josie's living room.

They tripped on acid for hours in McCarren Park and pointed out constellations while the day's heat settled.

Arthur took Josie to Beloved and saw the way Derek Blubbermann stared at her from across the room.

Arthur was happy the man complicit in so much of the drama in his life could see that he had moved on.

Arthur returned to the Spencer Street apartment for one night because Josie had to stay overnight with the children she nannied for in Harrison.

When Arthur walked out of the elevator, Leslie was in the kitchen, wearing a robe, pouring a glass of wine.

"I'm having trouble not being the most important woman in your life," said Leslie.

"Leslie, you'll always be important to me, but you know that we will never work together," said Arthur. "It's really for the best that we both move on."

Arthur sat down on the couch, exhausted from so many days on the road.

Leslie sat down next to him.

"Why haven't you been home?" she asked.

"I want to give you space before you move out."

"You've been with your girlfriend."

"That doesn't have anything to do with the fact that we still need to give each other space."

"I don't want space," said Leslie, inching closer.

Leslie tried to kiss Arthur. He turned his head.

"How the fuck do you think you can reject me? I'm the one who's been here through all your bullshit. I'm the one who saved you when you tried to kill yourself."

"Leslie, I'm dating someone else. I'm trying to be a good person for once."

"So you cheat on me our entire relationship, and this new girl gets you when you're faithful. That's not fair."

"It's not about what's fair, Leslie. I'm sorry for the way our relationship went. Remember, you cheated on me too. We need to leave all of that in the past."

"Okay, but can we just fuck one last time?"

"No, Leslie. Absolutely not."

"Come on, Arthur," Leslie said, rubbing her hand on Arthur's thigh. "You think you're such hot shit because of your little parties and your stupid Rake story."

"No. I'm serious," he said, moving her hand away from his thigh. "We can't do this again."

"One last time," said Leslie. "Please."

"No. I'm not trying to hurt your feelings. I really care about you, but we can't have sex. I'm sorry."

"You really don't want me anymore?" Leslie said, moving her hand back to Arthur's thigh then to the crotch of his pants. "You don't love me?"

"I don't want to have sex with you. There's no reason for you to take it personally."

"Arthur, this will be the last time," she said, unzipping his pants. "I swear."

"Please don't do this," said Arthur.

Leslie took Arthur's dick out from the open fly of his pants and put it in her mouth.

"Please stop, Leslie. I don't want to do this."

"Last time, I promise," she said, quickly maneuvering to sit on top of him.

Leslie continued without Arthur's consent. She took sex from Arthur that night. She raped him.

Arthur spent the next day at work distraught. He sent Leslie confrontational texts about how she had raped him.

"Women can't rape men," said Leslie. "And if you tell your girlfriend that I raped you, you will look stupid."

Arthur made plans to meet Josie at a concert at Bowery Ballroom later that night.

When Arthur arrived at Bowery Ballroom, he saw Leslie at the bar with co-workers from *Abstract*.

She rushed up to him, holding a glass of whiskey instead of wine.

"I'm sorry about last night."

"It's fine, Leslie."

"I was in a dark place. I was drunk. It's hard for me to see you move on and be happy while I just sit at that apartment and get drunk alone."

"That's not an excuse for what you did, but whatever. Josie is coming here. I don't want any drama."

"She's coming here?"

"Yes, Leslie."

"Why are you parading her all over town?"

"Leslie, we're broken up. Stop policing my every move. I'm allowed to take someone to a concert."

"Are you going to tell her that I raped you?"

"I'm going to tell her what happened."

Arthur got a text from Josie that said she was walking up to the venue. He went outside to meet her.

Josie moved up Delancey Street with elegance. She wore heels, a black dress, and a leather jacket.

Arthur met Josie with open arms in front of the venue. He briefly forgot about the dispute with Leslie.

"How was your day, baby?" said Arthur.

"Better now that I'm with you," said Josie.

Leslie popped up outside just as Arthur and Josie were kissing and watched from ten feet away, ripping a cigarette with more vigor than usual, seething.

"I fucked him last night!" Leslie yelled.

Arthur and Josie turned to look. Leslie had already jumped into a cab.

"Who is that?" asked Josie.

"That's my ex," said Arthur.

"What is she talking about?"

"She raped me last night."

Josie's smile became a scowl. Her shoulders slumped. Her soul sank to the bottom of her heels.

"How does that happen?" asked Josie.

"I was about to tell you. I told her that I was going to tell you. That's why she came out here."

"Why is she here anyway?"

"Because this industry, this world, is ridiculous. Everyone goes to the same parties and fucks the same people, and I'm so happy you're not a part of that."

"But how did she rape you?"

"We were on the couch. She wanted to have sex. I told her no a million times. I told her I have a girlfriend. She kept trying over and over and she wore me down. She reached into my pants and took my dick out and put it in her mouth and got on top of me. And, it's like, what am I going to do at that point? Fight her? She already said that she would lie about me hitting her. She raped me."

"Fucking bitch," said Josie.

"She's crazy," said Arthur. "I know every guy says their ex is crazy, but she's actually crazy."

"Why didn't you tell me sooner?"

"Because I knew I was seeing you tonight. I wanted to look you in your eyes and tell you in person."

"So now I just have to live with this?"

"No, fuck her. She's mad that I'm happy with you. She wants to ruin my life and yours. We are never going to let her lies affect what we have going on between us. I love you. I'm sorry that this happened. I hope that you can understand and forgive me."

"I love you too, Arthur. It's not your fault."

Arthur touched Josie's face and she did the same to his. They stared into each other's eyes before closing them and kissing against the wall outside of the venue.

Arthur stayed with Josie and did not see Leslie for a week after the Bowery Ballroom incident.

Then he went home to Spencer Street in hopes of packing enough clothes to avoid Leslie during the three weeks she had left living in the apartment.

Leslie was home when Arthur arrived. She tore into him as soon as he stepped out of the elevator.

"Your new girlfriend is a fucking basic idiot and I'm tired of you posting pictures of her on Twitter. I've gotten texts from literally everyone we know asking who she is and it's tacky. Show some respect."

"Leslie, I don't give a fuck about any of those people," said Arthur, setting his phone and wallet down on the kitchen counter. "You can have them all. Tell them to get a life and stop stalking my page."

"No one stalks your page, Arthur. They don't have to. Every time they look at their phone there's a new picture of you and your fucking nanny. No one cares."

"Clearly, you do," said Arthur, taking off his backpack and dropping it to the floor.

"Because I know that's your fantasy to meet someone and fall in love right away," said Leslie. "I know you're happy right now, and she's tall and skinny and pretty, but I don't want you to forget about me."

"I already did," said Arthur. "Get over it. Go fuck Derek Blubbermann or something."

Leslie grabbed Arthur's phone off the counter and threw it at the floor, cracking the screen.

When Arthur went to pick up his phone, Leslie snatched his debit card and ID out of his wallet and tried to break them in half.

Arthur wrestled his debit card and ID away from Leslie. They fell to the floor during the struggle.

When they got up from the floor, Leslie punched Arthur in the jaw and spit in his face.

Arthur wiped the spit from his face and picked up his backpack. He left the kitchen and called the elevator.

The elevator opened.

Arthur stepped onto the elevator.

"I'm bleaching your clothes!" yelled Leslie.

Leslie grabbed a bottle of bleach and ran to the bedroom. Arthur chased her into the bedroom.

Leslie was in the walk-in closet. Arthur knocked the bottle of bleach out of her hands.

The bottle of bleach fell to the ground. Its contents spilled onto the hardwood floor.

Leslie ripped Arthur's shirts off of their hangers. Arthur grabbed her denim jacket from behind and pulled a flailing Leslie away from the closet, into the bedroom.

Arthur used too much force when he pulled Leslie away from the closet. Leslie lost her balance.

She fell to the floor face first.

The impact cut open her chin.

Thick pools of crimson blood soaked the black rug in the bedroom.

NINE

The cut on Leslie's chin required twelve stitches.

Arthur waited outside of the emergency room. He spoke to Leslie's mother on the phone.

"Leslie tried to bleach my clothes," said Arthur. "I pulled her away from the closet and she fell. It was a freak accident. I'm so sorry."

"You and Leslie can't be together anymore," said Leslie's mother.

"We've been broken up for a while. I never even come home. The first time I did in a week, we fought."

"Are you at the hospital yet?"

"Yes. I registered with Leslie. Now I'm waiting. She's with the doctors."

"How bad is it?"

"We're in the middle of everything now. The first comment from the doctor was that it won't be very bad. They haven't done the stitches yet."

"Okay. Thank you, Arthur."

"I'm sorry, Mrs. Nostril. This is so sad."

"It is sad, Arthur. I think, after this, you both should realize and understand that you need to get away from each other. It's not healthy, mentally or physically."

"I just want you to know that it was an accident. I never wanted this to happen."

"I know, Arthur. I've met you enough times to know that you're a good person. Don't beat yourself up over this. Leslie is no angel. She drinks too much, and she's not innocent, but no one deserves stitches."

"I completely agree. And I promise you that I will pay for the hospital bills and do anything that's necessary to help either of you in this situation."

Arthur sat on the ground outside of the emergency room and chain-smoked cigarettes to calm his nerves. He considered putting out one of the cigarettes on his arm to inflict physical pain on himself.

Arthur wished that he had let Leslie destroy every item of clothing he owned. Anything would be better than the despair he felt at that moment.

What happened on Spencer Street the hour before was not intentional, but Arthur was a black man who showed up to the hospital with a bleeding white woman. He knew the narrative could be manipulated. He knew Leslie had, in her mind, reason to be vindictive.

He lit another cigarette and waited for police to show up and take him away in handcuffs.

Police never showed up.

Arthur drove Leslie home from the hospital. She was relatively tranquil about the incident.

"The doctors asked me if the cut was a result of domestic abuse," Leslie said, as Arthur's car cruised down Myrtle Avenue. "I didn't press charges because it was an insane situation, and we both overreacted."

"I'm so sorry," said Arthur. "I told your mother that I will pay for the hospital bills."

"The most important thing is that we stay away from each other forever," said Leslie. Tears ran down her face to the white gauze covering the stitches on her chin.

"I agree," said Arthur. "If you ever need help with anything, I'm still here for you."

"My face is fucked, and, for the rest of my life, when I see this scar, I'll think of you. That's enough."

Arthur and Leslie returned to the Spencer Street apartment as the sun rose, as they had done many times.

Leslie sent an email to her *Abstract* co-workers and said that she would not be coming into work that day. She went to sleep in the same outfit she wore to the hospital.

Arthur got a wet rag and cleaned up the blood and bleach that had soaked into the bedroom floor.

The last time Arthur saw Leslie was the day she moved out of the apartment on Spencer Street.

Arthur spent the three weeks after the incident at either Josie or Manny's apartments. On the rare occasion that neither apartment was available, Arthur slept in his chair at the Sounds office.

During those three weeks, the first hospital bill for Leslie's stitches arrived. Arthur sent Leslie's mother six hundred twenty-six dollars to cover the bill.

Leslie was supposed to be completely moved out by the last day of May. Thunderstorms and flash floods in Brooklyn interrupted the move.

When Arthur went home on the first day of June, he was surprised to find Leslie standing at the kitchen counter, opening a bottle of red wine, surrounded by a small collection of moving boxes.

The stitches were gone but a scar remained.

"I didn't expect to see you here," said Arthur.

"My boys from Buffalo moved almost everything yesterday," said Leslie. "Then the rain started. I'm here now to get the last boxes. My roommate is coming over with his car in thirty minutes."

"Why do you have wine?"

"To celebrate. I'm going to miss this place."

"Nothing good ever happened at this apartment."

Leslie poured two glasses of wine. "We need to talk about my security deposit."

Arthur unzipped his backpack and took out his checkbook. "I know. I owe you six hundred."

"Arthur, I want at least a thousand."

"You gave me six hundred at the beginning of April. Then you lived here rent-free the last six weeks of your stay. Four weeks of that is your last month's rent. Two weeks of that is half of your security deposit. I owe you six hundred. Don't try to scam me."

"I'm not trying to scam you, Arthur. You fucked up my chin. I need more than six hundred dollars."

"I just sent your mother money for the first bill. I will send her more for the next. None of that has anything to do with your security deposit."

"Arthur, write me a check for twelve hundred dollars or I will tell everyone what you did."

"You're extorting me now?"

"Write the fucking check. I know you have it. Stop being a cheap piece of shit and at least be fair with me when I'm moving out."

"This isn't fair at all."

Arthur begrudgingly wrote Leslie a check for six hundred dollars more than what he owed her.

Arthur slid the check across the counter to Leslie.

"There," he said. "You happy? Can you pack the rest of your shit and leave now?"

"Have a final drink with me," she said, pushing one of the wine glasses to Arthur's side of the counter.

"No, Leslie. I'm scared."

"Scared of what?"

"Fighting."

"No fighting, Arthur. I promise."

"You should've told me you were here. I would've waited until you left."

"Oh, I forgot, you're a cokehead. I should've brought cocaine."

Arthur turned around and walked to the elevator.

"Wait, I'm sorry," said Leslie. "Don't go."

"Why do you have to insult me?" said Arthur, walking back to the kitchen counter.

"Why did you have to fuck up my chin?"

"I knew you were going to start blaming this on me. First, it was an accident. What are you telling people now? That your nigger boyfriend beat you?"

"Arthur, everyone knows I instigate the fights, and I have not left out my role in what happened, but you're still responsible for this. You don't get to go and live a happy life while my face is fucked up. That book? Forget about it. Stop writing. Stop tweeting. You don't exist in this industry anymore after what you did to me."

"You wouldn't have a fucking job if it wasn't for me. I introduced you to everyone. I made you."

"You did not make me, Arthur."

"Leslie, Boris did not want to hire an intern who was fucking multiple people on staff. I told him that was bullshit. I vouched for you. I'm not saying you owe me anything, but stop acting like I didn't put you on."

"You didn't. I worked for what I have. I'm the one who's a hundred thousand dollars in debt because I got my master's degree. Did you even finish school?"

"Fine. You don't have to give me credit for helping your career. But you need to take responsibility for your actions in this most recent incident."

"I have taken responsibility."

"No, Leslie, you haven't. Bleaching clothes, breaking phones and debit cards, hitting people, and spitting in people's faces isn't normal. You played a serious role in what happened to your chin, but you love to act like the entire situation was my fault."

"I haven't told anyone this was your fault, but people deserve to know that you're not a good person."

"You say that like you're some kind of saint. You did me wrong too."

"Of course I did, Arthur. You treated me like shit our entire relationship. You made a big deal about Derek, when you've slept with more people on the side than I even know about. You called me a bitch and a whore and you made me mentally unstable."

"I apologize for all of that, but stop playing the victim. You were nasty too. Tell people whatever you want, as long they know the cut on your chin was the result of an accident. I can already tell you're about to spin it like your big, black, scary boyfriend beat you."

"Arthur, I wouldn't do that."

"You need to tell people that we treated each other like shit and now we've moved on. You go do your thing, and I will do mine."

"See, that's what I have a problem with. You don't get to work in this industry anymore. You need to move somewhere quiet and disappear."

"That's not going to happen."

"Arthur, I'm serious. If I see your byline on another article, or you DJ another party, or you continue to try getting a book deal, or you post another photo of your nanny on Twitter, it's not going to be pretty."

That comment reminded Arthur that, earlier, Josie said that she would come straight to Spencer Street when she was finished working in Harrison. She wanted to celebrate Arthur's first night in the apartment alone.

Arthur pulled out his phone and started to text Josie to not come over because Leslie was there.

Josie buzzed Arthur's apartment at that very moment. The intercom system's black-and-white video feed showed her standing outside of the building.

"Who is that?" asked Leslie.

Arthur did not answer.

Leslie ran to the other side of the counter.

"Hi," said Leslie, into the intercom.

"Hi?" said Josie, on the other end.

Leslie canceled the intercom call.

"You invited her to our home," said Leslie. "That's so disrespectful. That changes everything."

"It's my apartment now," said Arthur. "I can invite over whoever I want."

"You couldn't even wait one day before you brought the nanny over. You're disgusting."

"You really should've told me that you were going to be here. I have to go."

"You're leaving me on my last day in the apartment to go be with her?"

"Yes, Leslie. I support you being with whoever you want to be with. Stop trying to control me."

"I'm going to fuck everyone this summer and you're going to regret leaving me."

"No, I won't. I'll be happy for you."

"I'm serious about you disappearing, Arthur. Your New York City privileges are over."

Arthur's phone rang with a call from Josie.

"Is that her?" asked Leslie.

Arthur did not answer Leslie's question. He went to the balcony to take the call alone.

"Hey, baby," said Arthur.

Josie was in her car on Spencer Street, directly in front of Arthur's apartment building. She contemplated leaving when she heard another woman answer Arthur's intercom but figured that she would call him first.

"Who was that on your intercom?" asked Josie, in an uncharacteristically indignant tone.

"That psycho came here," said Arthur. "I'm coming downstairs right now. Please wait for me."

Arthur went from the balcony back into the apartment and called the elevator.

"I'm leaving," Arthur said, to Leslie. "Good luck with the rest of your move."

"That's it. I'm filing a police report tonight and tweeting the photo," said Leslie. "You're done. Enjoy your nanny because that's all you're going to have left."

The elevator opened.

"And I'll post the video of you saying that you'll lie about me hitting you and get away with it because you're white," said Arthur.

"You want to get petty?" said Leslie. "Great. We can ruin each other's lives. But it's over for whatever little career you think you have right now. I feel sorry for Josie because she doesn't even know what's coming."

"Goodbye, Leslie. Have a nice life."

Arthur was overcome with grief. When he told Josie what happened in the apartment, she took him to Tap House on Myrtle Avenue to cheer him up.

Arthur cried in the bathroom of the bar when he thought about how Josie would be negatively affected by dating him, but he needed her.

Leslie did not file a police report that night or tweet a photo of the cut on her chin.

Arthur put every experience with Leslie to the back of his mind and went on to have the best summer of his life.

He spent practically every minute of that summer with Josie. Their honeymoon phase never ended.

Josie and Leslie were both from upstate New York, and they were both Cancers, born within two weeks of each other, but that's where the comparisons stopped.

Josie had never been blackout drunk in her life. Leslie got blackout drunk twice every weekend.

Josie started a club called the Sunshine Committee in high school. The club's purpose was to spread joy throughout the school. They sent Sunshine Grams to bullied students who sat alone at lunch. Leslie bullied her peers in high school.

Josie was a peppy, optimistic young woman. Leslie's outlook was sardonic.

Arthur romanticized hedonism, and Leslie was the perfect partner with whom to explore the darkest corners of his soul, but that era had ended.

Josie taught Arthur how to love again.

Arthur and Josie made love more times in June than he and Leslie did during their entire relationship. Josie went on birth control because she knew that if she got pregnant with Arthur's child she would keep it.

Josie loved calling boys "dad." She called Arthur "dad." She called Arthur's friends "the dads." She called Arthur's apartment "Dad Pad." And, of course, Josie was "mom," and Josie's friends were "the moms."

Arthur and Josie's name for her bed at the Linden Street apartment was "the Cloud." It was an elevated bed that they had to climb on and off, with room underneath for armchairs, a bookshelf, and a jewelry stand.

They spent many nights on the Cloud naked, talking, smoking a joint as the sun rose.

One night, Arthur and Josie were on the Cloud, smoking a joint, coming down from acid, and Arthur could not grasp why Josie loved him.

Arthur's ego was a blanket for his equally outsized insecurities. He had delusions of grandeur and thought himself a mad genius whose writing would change the world, but, in the same breath, he thought of himself as depraved, pedestrian, and ugly.

Josie did not think Arthur was ugly. She caught herself staring at him often, including that night on acid.

"You're the hottest guy I've ever seen," said Josie.

"You don't mean that," said Arthur.

"I'm serious. Why do you think I walked up to you at that party? I was checking you out the entire night. And then I told Vera, 'There's that cute writer boy,' and you know how Vera is. She was like, 'Okay, Josie. If you want to talk to him then go talk to him.'"

Josie passed Arthur the joint as the sun brought Linden Street to life.

"I was so nervous that night," said Arthur. "I drove home the next day mad at myself for not making a move on you. You had a boyfriend, though. Would you have even done anything with me that night?"

"Oh my God, I was waiting for you to make a move the whole time," said Josie. "I would've cheated on that weenboy in two seconds."

"It's better that we didn't cheat on our exes that night. It would've started our relationship the wrong way. I'm glad we waited until we could be with each other."

"I know. It's so much better this way. Earlier this year, when I was breaking up with my ex, my brother-in-law told me, 'Move to New York and find your husband.' And I feel like I really did."

Arthur put out the joint. The acid was only just tapering off. Arthur legitimately wondered if Josie was real.

"I can't believe you actually like me," said Arthur.

"Are you kidding?" said Josie. "I love you. I thought you were too cool for me. I thought you were going to hit it once and disappear."

Josie laid her head on Arthur's chest.

"That's the same shit I was thinking," said Arthur. "I was like, 'I'm lucky enough to get this tonight, and it's a blessing from God, but I'm going hit her up tomorrow and she's going to be like, 'Sorry, that was a mistake. I'm way too hot for you.'" And that would've been fine."

Josie lifted her head off Arthur's chest and looked into his eyes. She stroked his face.

"Arthur, you're amazing. You're brilliant. You're beautiful. I want to fuck you and suck your dick every time I see you. One day, I want to have your babies. You're the most fun person I've ever been with. You literally make me feel like a princess."

"You have to be a hallucination," said Arthur. "You can't be real."

Leslie was physically out of Arthur's life, but she was no less menacing in text. Leslie used text messages to harass Arthur all summer.

When Arthur posted a photo of Josie at Manny's Massachusetts lake house on Independence Day, he got a text from Leslie: "I told you about posting pictures of Josie. We get it. You have a new girlfriend. If you don't start acting respectful, I'm pressing charges."

The next day, Leslie texted Arthur: "Come on. Get rid of this girl and go to therapy with me."

Arthur ignored both texts.

When Arthur posted a photo of himself and Rake at Senator's Ball music festival, he got a text from Leslie: "I know you're backstage, but just remember that you're not special. You're a disgusting human being, and if I see you or that bitch at Senator's Ball, I will cause a scene."

The next day, Leslie texted Arthur: "God, I miss you. You're my soul mate."

Arthur ignored both texts.

When the Book Club threw another party in July, Arthur got a text from Leslie: "I'm cutting off everyone who goes to your parties and telling them what you did. The only reason people come to your parties is because it's fun to watch a train wreck. You don't look cool standing on tables dancing. You look like a drug addict and an idiot. I will be contacting the owners of Kinfolk tonight."

The next day, Leslie texted Arthur: "Look, I'm just upset because my second cover story came out and I didn't have anyone to celebrate with. All I wanted to do was see you and make fun of everyone in the industry."

Arthur ignored both texts.

When Arthur released a line of T-shirts with *Walk in Like I'm Arthur Simon* written across the front, he got a text from Leslie: "Are the profits from your T-shirts going to my hospital bill?"

The next day, Leslie texted Arthur: "I'm sorry. Congratulations on the shirt. I've come to terms with how mutually abusive our relationship was, and, though it will take time for me to get over what happened to my chin, I know it was an accident and the result of a toxic relationship that went on too long. My parents are getting divorced and I just feel so sad. I'm thinking of you because I went to a Yankees game and I saw this young couple with these cute kids in the front row. That would've been us. We would've taken over the world."

Arthur ignored both texts.

He ignored every single text message Leslie sent that summer. When Leslie sent Arthur a photo of a second hospital bill for three hundred fifty dollars, he ignored that because she had already stolen six hundred dollars from him when she moved out.

Arthur knew that not responding to Leslie would inspire her to change the story about the cut on her chin and make herself an innocent victim. Whatever it took to get revenge for him letting her down so callously.

Arthur wanted to tell someone on the scene his side of the story.

Arthur stopped being friends with music writers after he broke up with Leslie. Those were Leslie's people now, and Arthur was glad to let her have them.

The only music writer who Arthur still had any semblance of a relationship with was Maggie Harvey.

One night, when Josie was upstate visiting her family in Ithaca, Arthur reached out to Maggie.

"Maggie, it's been a while," he texted. "Hope you're good. We should catch up."

"Wow, I was about to text you the same thing," she replied. "I've been going through some shit and I want to talk to you too."

"Tonight?" asked Arthur.

"Yeah. Give me a second. And do you have weed? I'm out. I'll bring something to drink."

Maggie showed up to Arthur's apartment with a bottle of whiskey. Arthur had weed. They hugged.

Nearly three years had passed since the two times Arthur and Maggie had sex. No sexual energy remained. They got along for more straightforward reasons. They were both from Chicago, listened to the same music, and had a similar sense of humor.

"This place is all yours now?" asked Maggie.

"Yeah, Leslie moved out," said Arthur.

"That's done?"

"It's over."

"That's good for both of you."

"It really is. I'm happier than ever."

"I see," said Maggie. She put her purse on the counter and pulled the whiskey out of a black plastic bag. "Tell me about this new girl all over your timeline."

"I'm in love right away. She's perfect."

"She's hot. I've seen the pictures."

"She's so hot. I'm shocked that she's dating me."

"Well, you do have the whole Arthur Simon thing going on right now."

"What do you mean?"

"The Book Club is the best party in New York. Your Twitter is hilarious. I even overheard strangers at Backstage Festival talking about your Rake story."

"What were they saying?"

"They said that the writing wasn't good."

"Fuck them."

"But I was just like, 'Damn, Arthur is iconic.' He's got these corny white boys riled up."

"Yeah, but I met Josie before all of that. She's not thirsty. She doesn't even have Twitter."

Arthur and Maggie took a few shots and smoked a few bowls. They gossiped. Maggie wanted to hear the story about how Arthur punched Derek Blubbermann.

Naturally, that topic brought the conversation back to Leslie.

"Leslie's awesome," said Maggie. "I love that girl."

"She's getting cover stories now. Killing it," said Arthur. "I really wish her the best."

"Do you still talk to her?"

"I don't. She texts me and I never respond, but it's no ill will. We just both need to move on."

"She needs to be free and experience being single and have her hoe phase."

"Exactly," said Arthur. "She told me she was going to fuck everyone, trying to make me jealous, but I was like, 'Please do.' That would be great for her. But enough about me. What's going on with you?"

Maggie was going through a divorce and needed to vent. They took the whiskey to the balcony. They sat and smoked cigarettes. Maggie told Arthur that, in addition to the divorce, she was raped on a trip to Los Angeles. Arthur listened intently. He did not speak except to agree with her points or offer his condolences.

Two hours passed.

Arthur and Maggie went back inside. She got her purse and told him to hold on to the rest of the whiskey.

"Maggie, wait," said Arthur. "There's one last thing that I wanted to talk to you about."

"Yeah, sure. What is it?"

"Before Leslie moved out, we had a bad fight."

"You two had a lot of those."

"This was the worst one we ever had."

"What happened?"

"We were arguing and she tried to bleach my clothes. I pulled her away from the closet and she fell and hit her chin and had to get stitches and it sucks."

"Wow."

"It was an accident. Leslie's said it was an accident. But I know she's going around saying I beat her. I just wanted somebody to know the truth."

"That's tough."

"What do you think is going to happen?"

"Certain people won't believe you and will never take your side on anything ever again, but you'll be fine. Shit happens. Most people understand that."

"I hope so. These racist motherfuckers can take that scenario and spin it any way they want to as soon as they have a grudge against me."

"Don't worry about it. You moved on. Leslie will move on. I know you're a good dude."

"Thank you," said Arthur. He hugged Maggie. "I really wish you the best with everything you're going through. Hit me up if you need anything."

"Trust me, I will," said Maggie, stepping onto the elevator. "Friends for life."

The elevator closed.

Arthur finished the whiskey alone.

Arthur became close friends with Rake that summer.

Their friendship peaked when Rake beefed with Bleek Bill, a rapper who publicly accused Rake of using ghostwriters, and boyfriend of Rake's ex, Vicki Menage.

Rake recorded a diss aimed at Bleek Bill and sent Arthur an early version of the song one night in late July.

"What do you think about that line, 'I just bought like twenty pairs of Nike gloves'?" Rake asked, over text.

"It's hard," said Arthur. "It lets Bleek know that you'll get into some street shit if he wants to take it there."

"I don't want that," said Rake. "Up here, shooters buy Nike gloves when they're about to pop off. That's not the message that I'm trying to send."

"You should say it," said Arthur. "It's a battle."

"Nah, I got the perfect line. I'm going to change it to something about how this is for the people who think that I don't write enough. Something like that."

Rake worked on the song for the rest of the night. By the time he finished, it was 5:00 a.m.

"Should I drop it tomorrow night?" asked Rake.

"No. Drop the song right now," said Arthur. "Tweet 'Scary hours' before you do it."

"You know what's the craziest part?"

"What's that?"

"I live in the Four Seasons when I'm in Toronto," said Rake. "Bleek and Vicki had a concert here last night. They're in the room directly below me right now."

Rake released the song shortly after 5:00 a.m. The song had the intended effect. Rake was instantly crowned the victor in the battle with Bleek Bill.

Internet users created thousands of memes that made fun of Bleek Bill for his loss. Rake spent the entire day sending Arthur screenshots of his favorite memes.

Arthur went to Toronto the following weekend.

Rake was hosting the annual Owl Festival in his hometown. The Book Club was throwing its first international party. The promoter paid for Arthur's flight. Josie drove up with Ryan and Aaron later that night.

Arthur texted Rake on his first day in Toronto. "I'm in your city. What's up?"

"I'm doing rehearsal at the venue," Rake replied. "Come through."

When Arthur arrived at the venue, Rake sat down and took a break. His Jordan sneakers dangled in mid-air off the front of the stage. Arthur stood on the floor.

"Dog, you want to know how the whole ghostwriter shit started?" said Rake.

"Of course," said Arthur.

"Bleek approached the kid who wrote for me to write for him. The kid was like, 'Nah, I'm down with Rake right now, so I'm sticking with him.' Bleek felt disrespected and figured he would try to expose me."

"How are you addressing the beef at the festival?"

"You know all the memes that we've been sending back and forth?"

"Yeah. Some of them are so ridiculous."

"When I perform the diss, we're putting all the best memes on the screen behind me," Rake said, pointing to the Jumbotron that crewmembers were installing.

"That's the nail in the coffin. I mean, you already killed dude, and the Internet has been wild all week, but having the festival right now is insane."

"I don't even feel good about it," said Rake. "This shit is dark. I used to be friends with that man. But he's the one who switched on me, so I had to end him."

"He's making a big deal about how you wore his chain that one time," said Arthur.

"Bro, he came up to me at a basketball game and put the chain around my neck, talking about, 'You're family now.' I was sitting there laughing like, 'Do I give this shit back now or what?' He's a dumb ass nigga."

"How did you even get in a position to have people saying you have ghostwriters?"

"I had people around me when I was recording the mixtape. There would be people in different rooms working on songs. I tried to record the way Kanye does."

"Honestly, I don't think there's anything wrong with recording like that."

"That's what I'm saying. And if this battle has to be the vessel through which we can have a conversation about this and, maybe, change things, then so be it. With that said, I'm never working with ghostwriters again."

"Yeah, the pressure is on. You have to lock yourself in a room and write the next album by yourself."

"Exactly. I have to. I'm not asking anybody for help, opinions, none of that. And I have to sell a million copies in the first week. That's how I win the war."

Josie, Ryan, and Aaron's drive from New York to Toronto took longer than expected. They went straight to the Book Club's party at Soho House when they got to the city.

Arthur was snorting cocaine off the trackpad on his laptop and so intoxicated that he had trouble standing in the DJ booth.

When Arthur woke up next to Josie in a room at the Radisson, he did not remember much from the party.

"Oh, you're awake," said Josie. "How nice of you to join the rest of us."

"What happened last night?" said Arthur.

"That's what I want to know."

"The last thing I remember was when you, Ryan, and Aaron showed up while I was DJing. I drank a lot, I did a lot of coke, and I took a Xanax."

"You looked horrible," said Josie. "You couldn't stand. It was scary. Don't do anything like that ever again."

"I won't."

"I mean it, Arthur. I love you to death, but I'll break up with you on the spot the next time you get fucked up like that. It's not safe. It's not cute."

Arthur's megalomaniacal needs were met at Owl Festival.

When he waltzed through the venue with Josie at his side, a young white woman approached him, said that she was a big fan, and asked for a picture.

When he stood in line for drinks, a young white man approached him, said, "Arthur Simon? I love your writing," and asked for a picture.

When he walked to his seat, a group of teenagers yelled his name from their chairs on the lawn and waved to get his attention.

Arthur checked Twitter and vainly searched his own name. Another dozen people had posted about seeing Arthur at the festival. Four said they were too nervous to say hi. Arthur felt his power growing. His heart swelled.

Leslie never reacted well to run-ins with Arthur's fans. She hated Arthur's hollow fame. She knew it was fleeting and trivial, and, secretly, Leslie wanted Arthur's hollow fame for herself.

Josie knew Arthur's fame was fleeting and trivial, but she was not threatened by it, nor did she want it for herself. She existed in a different world than Leslie.

Josie did not like when women approached Arthur in public, but, outside of that, she found his fame cute and fascinating. She loved Arthur. When she observed Arthur's energetic interactions with his fans at the festival, she understood why they loved him too.

But, yes, the festival.

Rake performed and disparaging Bleek Bill memes were plastered on the Jumbotron behind him as promised.

The response to Rake's stunt was divisive.

A large contingency of music writers thought that Rake's use of memes to dismantle Bleek Bill was cheap, lazy, and avoided the topic of how he had not written much of the music on his previous album.

Arthur saw Rake at the after-party.

Arthur was at the bar, drinking with Josie, Ryan, and Aaron. Ryan and Aaron had sat in a different section at the festival because they bought scalped tickets at the entrance. They had all reunited at the after-party when Rake texted Arthur, asking him to meet near the exit of Soho House so that they could talk.

Josie and Ryan had already met Rake and did not care to meet him again. Aaron had never met Rake and did not care to meet him a first time.

Arthur left the bar and went to meet Rake near the exit on the first floor.

Rake was standing against the wall, drinking alone.

"You think that was the right approach?" Rake asked. "What are people saying?"

"The consensus is obviously that you won the battle," said Arthur. "Some people are mad about the memes, but people are always mad."

"I feel like the fans got it," said Rake. "But the writers are going to have it out for me."

"Don't worry about it," said Arthur. "I'm probably going to write something."

Rake shook Arthur's hand. "I appreciate you."

Two black women appeared out of thin air and introduced themselves to Rake.

Arthur went back to the bar.

Two days later, Maggie Harvey published a piece for *Backstage* titled "I'm Breaking Up With Rake."

Maggie's piece capitalized on the growing backlash against Rake.

She echoed sentiments that Rake had been cheap and lazy in his use of memes in the battle with Bleek Bill. The piece also lashed out at Rake as sexist for insinuating that Bleek was less of a man because his girlfriend, Vicki Menage, was more successful.

Everyone who was sick of Rake rallied behind Maggie's piece and relished in her digs at his tactics. Her piece was propped up as important and necessary criticism.

Rake got wind of Maggie's story.

"You see the *Backstage* piece?" Rake texted Arthur, who was back in Brooklyn by then.

"Yeah, I know that girl," said Arthur. "It's trash."

"I stopped reading after she admitted to having a Skrillex haircut," said Rake. "It's annoying that people actually get behind bitter bullshit like this."

"I'm writing a response right now," said Arthur. "It's going to address everything. I'll handle it."

The next day, Arthur published a piece for *Record* titled "The Rake Backlash Is Boring."

Arthur's piece capitalized on the backlash to the Rake backlash.

He called out the anti-Rake contingency for their selective outrage and hypocrisy in holding Rake to politically correct standards to which they did not hold other rappers.

Rake texted Arthur: "Fantastic piece. Thank you. This sets up the next album perfectly."

"That was just my honest reaction to everyone hating you all of a sudden," said Arthur. "I would have written the same story even if I didn't know you."

"I know," said Rake. "That's why I loved it."

Most notable about Arthur's piece was its thinly veiled personal attacks on Maggie. He used specific observations about Maggie's affinity for other rappers who could also be classified as sexist to make a point about the fickle nature of her feminist Rake critique.

Maggie texted Arthur to let him know that she was not upset by his piece and enjoyed the back-and-forth.

"It's so funny how we are the only two writers who can make these kinds of waves," she said.

"Yeah, it's really fun," said Arthur. "We dictate the conversation."

"I'm on the roof of the Met, drinking wine, dying laughing because this Internet shit is too easy."

"I'm about to go to a mansion in the Hamptons with Josie for the weekend. We won."

"Meanwhile, everyone on Twitter is going to think we are, like, out to ruin each other. I love it."

Secretly, Maggie was fuming. Arthur had stolen her moment and, the more she thought about it, the more she did want to ruin him, by any means necessary.

Maggie unfollowed Arthur on Twitter—a formal disavowal of acquaintance. She appeared in photos with Leslie soon thereafter.

Josie had been off birth control since Independence Day because the hormonal changes were not sustainable.

Each morning, Josie carefully studied her body in the bathroom mirror in Arthur's apartment.

One morning at the end of August, Josie walked back to the bedroom, naked, and stood at the foot of the bed. Arthur was just waking up.

"Do you notice anything different about my body?" She cupped her chest. "Look at my breasts."

Arthur shook himself out of his post-sleep daze. Josie's breasts were larger than usual, engorged.

"Clearly, they're bigger," said Arthur.

"This happens when you're pregnant," said Josie. "They hurt. Touch them. Feel how hard they are."

Josie walked to the side of the bed. Arthur sat up and touched both of her breasts.

"Do you think you're pregnant?"

"I don't know." Josie turned to the side. "Does my stomach look bigger?"

"Not really."

"I feel dizzy, Arthur. Kind of lightheaded."

"I'll get you some water."

Arthur got out of bed and started walking with Josie towards the kitchen. Her stride was slow.

"It's becoming more like nausea. I think, wait—" Josie ran to the bathroom and vomited in the toilet.

Josie made an appointment for that morning at the Planned Parenthood clinic near her job in Harrison.

Arthur skipped work and went with Josie to Harrison. Josie showed her ID at the entrance. Patients had to be identified and buzzed in as a security measure.

Arthur and Josie hugged and kissed in the lobby.

Josie went in to see the doctor. Arthur read a gossip magazine in the waiting area.

Josie was with the doctor for five minutes.

She returned to the waiting area. "I'm ready."

He put down the magazine. "That was quick."

Arthur walked with Josie out of the clinic.

"What happened?" Arthur asked, as soon as they stepped into the sunlight.

"I'm seven weeks pregnant," said Josie.

Josie started crying. She held Arthur as tightly as she could in the middle of the parking lot.

"What are we going to do?" Josie asked, pressing her wet face against Arthur's chest.

"We're going to have an awesome kid," said Arthur, stroking her hair, staring into the distance.

TEN

Josie moved in with Arthur.

Josie told the parents of the children that she nannied for that she was pregnant. They fired her.

"Those fuckers ambushed me," said Josie, sprawling across the couch.

"You should sue them," said Arthur, eating leftover Thai food at the kitchen counter. "I'm pretty sure that firing you for being pregnant is illegal."

Josie grabbed the Xbox controller and pulled up Netflix. "They gave me three thousand dollars."

"They don't want their kids seeing you pregnant with a black man's baby before you're married," said Arthur. "You should've gotten ten thousand."

"I'm not good at talking about money. I don't know how to be cutthroat like you."

"That's okay. You teach the baby to be kind and gentle. I'll teach the baby to be cutthroat and aggressive."

Josie's pregnancy inspired Arthur to pursue the book deal.

Arthur's agent suggested that Arthur's proposal build upon the subject matter of his *Voyeur* article.

Arthur wrote a fifty-page proposal for a book titled *White Women.*

The proposal had chapters about the Duluth lynchings, the Tulsa riots, the Rosewood massacre, the Marion lynchings, the Scottsboro Boys, the murder of Emmett Till, the Ku Klux Klan's "First and Always Protect White Womanhood" slogan, the Central Park Five, and the Charleston church massacre.

Arthur also included a chapter about what he had learned from his relationship with Leslie Nostril.

Arthur wanted to show how purported protection of white women was historically used as a scapegoat for destroying innocent black men in America.

Seven publishers bit.

Arthur had a week of meetings.

Tim Goldberg, executive editor at Park Avenue Publishing, offered Arthur $135,000 for the book.

Arthur accepted the offer.

The Book Club had a show the day after he got the offer.

Five hundred people crowded Wythe Avenue trying to get into Kinfolk.

Arthur was coked out and kept screaming "I'm rich now" into the microphone in the DJ booth.

Arthur and Josie went to Chicago.

Arthur showed Josie his high school and the golf course in Riverside where he got his first job.

They ate deep-dish pizza at Gino's East. They ate Italian lemonade at Mario's. They held hands and walked along the shore of Lake Michigan.

Josie met Arthur's mother, father, and two sisters for the first time.

"We're having a baby," said Arthur.

Arthur's family was ecstatic about the baby.

Arthur and Josie went to Ithaca.

Josie showed Arthur her high school and the restaurant in college town where she got her first job.

They ate tofu wings at Northstar House. They ate ice cream at Sweet Melissa's. They held hands and walked along the shore of Cayuga Lake.

Arthur met Josie's mother, father, and two sisters for the first time.

"We're having a baby," said Josie.

Josie's family was ecstatic about the baby.

Arthur announced his book deal.

He had not signed a contract, but Tim Goldberg told him that the deal was set in stone.

Derek Blubberman received the *White Women* press release from Park Avenue Publishing.

Derek texted Arthur: "Just got a press release about you. Congrats."

Leslie Nostril received the *White Women* press release from Park Avenue Publishing.

Leslie texted Arthur: "Is your book cover going to be my scar? I'm not dealing with this. We're going to court. You're so fucking selfish. And you owe us money."

Leslie went to the Seventy-Ninth Precinct on Tompkins Avenue and filed assault, menacing, and harassment charges against Arthur the next day.

Arthur and Josie went to Los Angeles.

They stayed in Beverly Hills with Arthur's friend, Clancy Chambers, during their first week in the city.

Clancy Chambers was a wealthy Harvard graduate who quit his job at Goldman Sachs and moved to Los Angeles to write for a popular television series.

Clancy told Arthur to send him a screenplay.

Arthur told Clancy that he would send him a screenplay when he had one ready.

The Book Club had a show in Los Angeles.

Ryan Irving had moved back to Boston, and Aaron Riley had moved to Atlanta, but they both flew in.

The show was in a warehouse in South Central. A thousand people came. A camera crew interviewed Arthur and filmed a segment about him for a television series.

Arthur and Josie stayed at the Chateau Marmont during their second week in the city.

Sounds by Surgeon Tre paid for the room so that Arthur could work out of the Culver City office that week.

Arthur and Josie watched the blood moon from Mulholland Drive on their last day in the city.

Josie's sisters visited Arthur and Josie in New York City.

The four of them went to Brooklyn Hospital Center for the baby's first sonogram.

The baby was the size of a walnut. The baby's heartbeat was strong.

Josie and her sisters made quinoa, kale salad, and baked chicken at the Spencer Street apartment.

Arthur left the apartment and went to get cigarettes at the bodega on DeKalb Avenue.

Arthur got a call from Josie.

"There's a man knocking on our door," said Josie. "He said that he's with NYPD and he's looking for Arthur Simon. I told him to go away."

The detective left a business card in their mailbox.

Arthur went to New Orleans.

He stayed on the rapper Wolf Haley's tour bus because he was writing a story about Wolf for *Traction*.

Arthur rode the tour bus to Texas.

He interviewed Wolf Haley backstage after Wolf's performance in Dallas.

Arthur went to see the Kennedy Memorial on Main Street. He read every placard about Kennedy's assassination at the Sixth Floor Museum.

The Book Club had a show in Austin.

The promoter paid for Arthur's bus. Ryan and Aaron were not there. Arthur DJ'd alone.

Arthur got an email from his agent: "You around to talk?"

Arthur called his agent.

"Is the contract ready to sign?" said Arthur.

"The contract is on hold," said the agent.

"What do you mean?" said Arthur.

"A woman, Leslie Nostril, contacted Park Avenue Publishing and said that you beat her. They asked for proof. She said that charges have been filed. Tim Goldberg said that the claims seem fishy, and he believes that you're innocent, but the insurance team won't move forward with the deal until you're fully exonerated. Once that happens, he said that we can pick up where we left off. He did suggest that you think about doing a different book."

Arthur called Clancy Chambers.

He asked Clancy for a referral to the best lawyer that he knew in New York City.

Clancy referred Arthur to Alexandria Simmons.

Alexandria had a law degree from Columbia and an undergraduate degree from Yale.

Arthur called Alexandria.

"My rate is five hundred dollars per hour," said Alexandria. "My retainer is five thousand dollars."

"I need a week to get the money," said Arthur.

"The sooner the better," said Alexandria. "I will call the detective in the meantime."

Arthur called Clancy again the next day.

"Alexandria's retainer is five thousand dollars," said Arthur. "My girlfriend is pregnant. I'm strapped for cash. Is there any way I can borrow that money?"

"Sure," said Clancy. "What's your address?"

"One ninety-five Spencer Street. Apartment eight. Brooklyn, New York. Eleven two zero five."

"A check will be in your mailbox by next week," said Clancy. "I'm glad to help."

Arthur called Alexandria.

"The money is on the way," said Arthur.

"Good," said Alexandria.

"Any updates?"

"Yes, I spoke to the detective. He wants to ask you some questions. That means you will be arrested. What day can you go into the precinct?"

"I leave for Europe tomorrow," said Arthur. "I'll have to go in when I get back."

The Book Club had a show in Paris.

Arthur, Josie, Ryan, Aaron, and Manny landed at Charles de Gaulle on a Thursday in late October.

The tour manager got them cabs to Hotel ibis Paris Bastille Opera 11ème. It was a simple, economical hotel in the Eleventh Arrondissement.

The five of them ate baguettes and onion soup at a café in Le Marais. They bought fake fur coats for ten euro at a thrift shop on Boulevard Saint-Germain. They took photos in front of the Seine.

Arthur and Josie kissed under the Eiffel Tower.

Arthur posted a photo of himself and Josie under the Eiffel Tower. In the photo, Arthur had his hand on Josie's baby bump. Arthur captioned the photo with a "three-person family" emoji.

Leslie texted Arthur: "You're having a kid? Jesus Christ, Arthur. God bless you both. You will have a daughter, and you will regret what you did to me every time you look at her."

Arthur ignored Leslie's text.

Arthur and Josie had sex all over their hotel room before the show.

The show was at Le Pop-Up du Label.

Arthur and Josie reunited with Ryan, Aaron, and Manny at the restaurant above the venue. The table had a spread of well-aged cheese. Everyone ate steak. Josie even allowed herself a sip of the vintage red wine.

They went downstairs and took the stage.

The room was packed and sweaty and loud.

Arthur grabbed the microphone.

"We're here from America. I feel like this is 1944 and I'm liberating you guys right now."

The crowd moaned.

Ryan whispered to Arthur. "It's still too soon."

Arthur played a Rake song and the Parisians went back to jumping around in front of the stage.

Ryan wouldn't take off his fake fur coat. Aaron was off a Xanax, wearing Arthur's Wayfarers. Manny spilled whiskey on his Bruins jacket. Josie danced the entire time. Arthur kept diving into the crowd.

They smoked hash on the street with the Parisians after the show. They saw a man leaking pools of blood from his face to the pavement in front of a late-night creperie when they walked back to the hotel.

The tour manager got them coffee, croissants, and cabs to Gare du Nord in the morning.

The group was held at the British border for six hours.

Ryan told border police he had a show in London. Border police said that he did not have a performance license and detained him.

The officers saw who Ryan was traveling with and detained everyone except Josie.

"You don't have to wait with them, Miss Akers," said an officer. "You're free to go on to London."

"I'm pregnant," said Josie. "And obviously I'm going to stay with my boyfriend."

"Well, your boyfriend and his mates aren't likely to make it through," said the officer. "So think about it."

Arthur had a friend from Sounds, Casey Black, who lived in London and DJ'd on the side.

Arthur called Casey.

"We're stuck at the border," said Arthur. "These British motherfuckers are serious."

"Bruv, you can't be telling feds you're performing if it's a low key gig at a small venue," said Casey.

"I'm going to finesse us through the border, but I know they'll be watching our social media. If we DJ, they'll ban us from the U.K."

"Tell feds stop playing with man. I'll come to the bloody border myself innit."

"I need you to DJ tonight so we can technically say that we didn't perform. We'll just stand on stage and hype up the crowd. You actually know how to DJ, so it'll be better for everyone. I'll send you a list of songs."

"Send it fam. Probably have most songs anyhow. Just tell me when and where about the gig."

Arthur gave the tour manager Casey's email.

Border police came back with the group's passports and said they were being denied entrance to the United Kingdom.

"Sir, can I please talk to you for five minutes and explain the situation?" said Arthur.

"No," said the officer.

"Please. There's been a huge misunderstanding."

The officer looked at his watch.

"Okay, Mr. Simon. Five minutes."

The officer took Arthur to an interview room.

"Sir, we're not real DJs," said Arthur. "We don't have equipment. All we do is plug in our phones. It's like if someone chose the music playing at a pub."

"And you still need a license for that in the United Kingdom," said the officer.

"I know, which is why the show is canceled. The Book Club is not DJing tonight. I don't care about DJing. I'm a writer. This is something stupid that I do on the side. The reason that we need to go to London is because we already paid for flights from Heathrow to Copenhagen. That's expensive, sir. I don't want to put the people who invested in us in that position. If you allow us entry, we will honor your rules and we will not DJ."

"I get that, but once we let you and your mates pass the border, how do we know you won't go to the venue and DJ anyway? What are you going to do in the United Kingdom if you don't do this performance?"

"Sir, I haven't been to London in ten years. I was sixteen the last time I visited this beautiful country, and I was only here for one day. I barely remember London and I want to change that. I'm in awe of the United Kingdom. Without you guys, America wouldn't exist. All I want is a chance to see your country again. I miss it. You're asking what I would do—what *wouldn't* I do? I want to see Big Ben and Piccadilly Circus and Hyde Park. I want to walk the Tower Bridge and visit the Tower of London and go back to the Globe Theatre. I want to hold my pregnant girlfriend's hand on the banks of the Thames. I would move to London if I had the opportunity, sir. All I'm asking for is one night to experience the city."

Arthur stared into the officer's eyes.

The officer studied Arthur's passport.

"We will allow you to pass the border."

Arthur's anxiety vanished.

"Thank you so much," said Arthur.

"You're welcome," said the officer. "Please do not DJ in any form tonight. We will find out if you do."

"We absolutely won't, sir. Thank you."

"Welcome to the United Kingdom."

Arthur, Josie, Ryan, Aaron, and Manny took the Eurostar to St Pancras International in London. Night had fallen by the time they arrived.

The tour manager got them two London taxis to the Old Ship Inn in Hackney.

Aaron got an hour of sleep before the show. Ryan and Manny drank Boddingtons at the Victorian pub beneath their rooms. Arthur and Josie ate fish and chips at a table across from the bar.

Arthur went outside and smoked a Lucky Strike in front of the hotel.

Three young, white British boys in *Walk in Like I'm Arthur Simon* T-shirts ran up to Arthur on the street.

"Oh my God, it's really you," said one.

"I'm your biggest fan," said another.

"Thank you for coming to London. We've been waiting for this forever. We love you," said a third.

The show was at Moth Club.

Arthur kept his word. The Book Club did not DJ.

Casey Black was a professional and played a first-rate set. Three hundred British kids moshed for five hard hours and took photos of themselves with the Book Club. "Man Don't Care" created a rampage.

A British music magazine interviewed Arthur after the show. Aaron huffed nitrous oxide with fans on the street. Ryan and Manny went to the Scotch of St. James.

Josie and Arthur woke up early in the morning. They ate a full breakfast. Josie was a Harry Potter fanatic, so they went to Platform 9 ¾. They walked from King's Cross to Trafalgar Square. Arthur posted a photo of himself and Josie on the Waterloo Bridge.

Leslie texted Maggie: "I can't believe Arthur took that basic bitch to Europe."

Maggie responded: "She's not even cute. This Book Club shit is so corny."

Arthur and Josie took a London taxi back to the Old Ship Inn. Ryan, Aaron, Manny, and the tour manager were waiting in a black van on the cobblestone pavement behind the hotel. Arthur and Josie hopped in the van.

They made it to their gate at Heathrow as the final boarding call was announced.

The first destination in Copenhagen was Christiania, a self-governed village of anarchists on the east side of the city.

They went to Christiania and bought weed. The dealers were jumpy and wore facemasks. A sign on their stand read *No Photos* in red letters.

Manny rolled four joints at a stone table next to a dilapidated shack. An old white man emerged from the shadows of the village and screamed obscenities and murder threats at no one in particular.

The tour manager got cabs to the Square Hotel.

Aaron used the Wi-Fi to check his Twitter. Ryan and Manny drank whiskey at the hotel bar.

Arthur and Josie strolled the streets in search of food. They ate burgers at Modern American Diner and laughed at the photos of Williamsburg in the menu.

Arthur and Josie spent the hour before the show running around Tivoli Gardens. Halloween decorations covered the park. Josie paid twenty Danish kroner for a fresh caramel apple. Winding pathways evoked Lewis Carroll. They vowed to bring their child in the future.

The show was at Jupiter Club.

The club was in a dark alley in Indre By.

A go-go dancer tried to fight Josie because Josie stopped the dancer from coming in the DJ booth. Tension increased between the club owners and the Book Club. Arthur played "Wonderwall" and they were kicked out.

Ryan and Manny went to a strip club. Aaron went to sleep. Josie stopped Arthur from buying cocaine from Nigerians in track jackets in front of the hotel.

Every cab in Berlin was a cream yellow Mercedes.

The Book Club's cream yellow Mercedes passed the Victory Column on the way to the hotel. Arthur stared out of the window. He recognized the golden statue from documentaries about the Second World War.

Arthur and Josie dropped their bags at Hotel Vier Jahreszeiten and roamed the Kreuzberg streets.

They ate döner kebabs in Görlitzer Park and kissed on the banks of the Spree at East Side Gallery.

They wandered out of Kreuzberg and down Unter den Linden to Brandenburg Gate.

"I didn't see this last time I was here," said Arthur. "I always said I would come back. I can't believe I'm here a year later with you and we're having a baby. I love you."

"I love you too, Arthur. This trip is life-affirming. We're bringing our kid back to all of these cities one day."

They walked through the Memorial to the Murdered Jews of Europe. Josie cried as they made their way past the looming slabs of concrete.

The show was at Repeat Bar.

The crowd was decent.

Arthur, Josie, Ryan, Aaron, and Manny huddled in the DJ booth. They waxed poetic about how they would remember the Europe tour forever.

They did a photo shoot with a German fashion magazine at the Berlin Wall after the show.

The check from Clancy was not in Arthur's mailbox.

Arthur called Clancy.

"I just got home from Europe," said Arthur. "Are you still sending the check?"

"Unforeseen expenses came up," said Clancy. "I can't help you anymore. Sorry about that."

Alexandria called Arthur.

"Have you decided what day you want to meet with the detective?" said Alexandria. "And do you have the five thousand dollars for the retainer?"

"I don't want to do this at all so the date doesn't matter, but I can meet with him in three weeks. And I don't have the money. The person who was going to give me a loan can't do it anymore. I need a little more time."

"I'm not coming to Brooklyn to meet with the detective or putting my name in at court unless you pay me. You should've paid me before Europe. I've already put in five hours on your case. Please figure it out."

Arthur and Josie went to Ithaca.

They went to Cinemapolis on the Commons and saw *Goosebumps* on Halloween night.

They ate vegetable bibim bop with Josie's sisters at Asia Cuisine. They ate chicken tikka masala with Josie's mother and father at Diamond's.

Arthur laid with Josie in her childhood bed.

"I'm sorry for ruining your life," said Arthur.

"You haven't ruined anything," said Josie.

"You don't mean that."

"Yes, I do. I'm having your child. We're traveling the world. I'm happier than I've ever been."

"I'm getting arrested in two weeks, Josie."

"And I know you didn't do anything that you're being accused of. I saw Leslie. She's a mess. She's not going to win in court so I'm really not worried about it."

"I can't even afford a lawyer. I owe Alexandria twenty-five hundred. And I still have to pay the retainer."

"What happened to the check from Clancy?"

"He can't do it anymore."

"Why don't you ask your parents?"

"I'm not ready to tell them yet. I'm getting five thousand dollars from the *Traction* story. I need to find someone who will let me pay them back in, like, a month."

109

"I can ask my parents."

"Please don't. I don't want you to do that."

Josie told her mother that Arthur had been paying for everything since she lost her job, that his ex-girlfriend falsely accused him of domestic abuse, and that they needed to borrow five thousand dollars for a lawyer.

Josie's parents were not rich, but they had slightly more than five thousand dollars in their savings account.

Josie's mother wired payment for the retainer to Alexandria the next day.

Arthur and Josie went to Brooklyn Hospital Center for the baby's second sonogram.

The baby was the size of a grapefruit. The baby's heartbeat was strong.

"Do you want to know the sex?" said the sonogram technician.

"Yes," said Arthur and Josie, in near unison.

"Just checking," said the sonogram technician. "Some people don't like to know."

"We want to know," said Arthur.

"I want a girl, but I think it's a boy," said Josie.

"You got what you wanted," said the sonogram technician. "This is a girl."

Arthur and Josie ate burgers at Junior's after the sonogram. Arthur held her hand on the orange table while they shared a milkshake. Josie started crying.

"What's wrong?" said Arthur.

"Nothing," said Josie, wiping her tears, laughing.

Arthur was arrested for the first time in his life on the nineteenth of November.

He kissed Josie and stepped into the elevator in their apartment.

He met Alexandria in front of the apartment.

They met with the detective at 4:00 p.m.

Arthur stared into the detective's eyes.

"My client knows what this is about," said Alexandria. "He will not be speaking about the matter."

"That's fine," said the detective. "We have to book him and take him downtown. Night court goes until one in the morning. Small chance he gets out tonight."

The detective put Arthur in bright silver handcuffs, put him in a holding cell, took a photo of him in the holding cell, took him to the basement of the precinct, took his mug shot, took his fingerprints, put him in another holding cell, and took him to a white van that was waiting outside of the precinct in the heavy rain.

Arthur sat in the back of the van with eight other black men in bright silver handcuffs.

The officers took Arthur to the basement of the courthouse on Schermerhorn Street, took his mug shot, took his fingerprints, and took him to a nurse's office where he was asked if he needed medical attention.

"No," said Arthur.

The officers put Arthur in another holding cell.

Arthur waited in the holding cell for six hours until his name was called.

The officers took Arthur upstairs and put him in another holding cell behind the courtroom.

Arthur saw a centipede near the toilet in the cell. He paced the cell worried that his name would not be called by 1:00 a.m. and he would have to stay overnight.

Arthur's name was called at 12:51 a.m.

The officers took Arthur to the courtroom. Josie and Alexandria were in the courtroom waiting for him.

Arthur was arraigned and formally charged with assault in the third degree, menacing, and harassment. The prosecutor fumbled through stacks of paperwork.

"Your Honor, the defendant is a danger to the complainant," said the prosecutor. "The People request five thousand dollars bail."

"Your Honor, that's not acceptable," said Alexandria. "My client's girlfriend is pregnant. She's here in this courtroom. My client lives in Brooklyn. He works in Manhattan. He's here today. There's no reason to suggest that he won't come to future court dates."

The judge was a black woman.

Arthur stared into the judge's eyes.

"Defendant is released on his own recognizance," said the judge.

"Thank you, your Honor," said Alexandria.

Josie cracked a smile in her seat.

Arthur continued to stare into the judge's eyes.

"Arthur Simon, you are reminded that the complainant, Leslie Nostril, has a temporary order of protection," said the judge. "You are not to contact Leslie Nostril by phone, text, email, social media, through other persons, or any other form of communication whatsoever, even if you believe that this person wants you to contact them. You are not to go near Leslie Nostril's place of residence, place of business, or any other locations where you believe that she may be. If you violate the order of protection, you will be arrested again. Your first court date is on the fifteenth of January. Have a good night."

Arthur wanted to piss off Leslie Nostril and every music writer who believed what she said about him.

Arthur published his Wolf Haley story on *Traction*'s website the day after he was arrested. He tweeted: "Went on tour with Wolf Haley. Best story of the year. Fuck everyone who has a problem with me."

The Wolf Haley story did not spark the same level of conversation that Arthur's previous stories had. Most of the music writers heard rumors that Arthur beat Leslie and did not want to support him.

Leslie texted Maggie: "Arthur is out of line. Don't the editors at *Traction* know what he did to me?"

Maggie responded: "They will know soon. He has one more time to say something cocky on Twitter. I'm going to expose the fuck out of him."

Arthur and Josie had dinner with Josie's family in Ithaca the day before Thanksgiving. They had dinner with Arthur's family in Chicago on Thanksgiving. They flew to San Francisco the Saturday after Thanksgiving.

Arthur and Josie existed on an illusory plane during their three days in San Francisco. The city was a shield, a parallel universe where no misfortune awaited.

They stayed in North Beach with Arthur's friend Svetlana Malenkov, an old friend from business school.

Arthur had a set at Feels Festival in Oakland on that first night. Aaron Riley was there. Aaron's family lived in the Bay, so he was home for Thanksgiving, but one of his friends from Atlanta was performing at Feels too.

Arthur trolled a crowd of five thousand with songs by Avril Lavigne and Panic! at the Disco. Aaron and Josie danced around the stage for the hour Arthur played.

Arthur's set sparked controversy when Questlove posted footage of Arthur DJing at the festival with only his phone, without blends or transitions.

Twitter backlash set in.

The aux cord DJ economy collapsed.

The collapse did not affect Arthur immediately. He was with Josie. They were still in a separate, dreamlike realm, disassociated from what was unfolding in reality.

They spent Sunday exploring trails at Muir Woods on Mount Tamalpais. Josie and Arthur sat inside one of the larger redwoods for twenty minutes.

"I could stay here for forever," said Josie.

Josie took Arthur to the SS Jeremiah O'Brien on Monday. They spent four hours poring over every placard on the war ship, taking in views of Alcatraz and the skyline.

Arthur sat at one of the battle turrets on the deck.

"I need one of these for everyone in the industry."

They went to Baker Beach and held each other on the serpentine cliffs along the Pacific Ocean.

"Your big day's coming," said Josie. "How do you feel? Is this how you envisioned twenty-seven?"

"I'm twenty-seven tomorrow. Wow," said Arthur. "I always thought I would die at twenty-seven."

"Don't say that. You will make it out of the next year alive. You will grow old with me and your daughter."

"You know, I think I figured out a name for her."

"That's trippy because so did I. I didn't bring it up because I'm scared that you won't think it's good."

"Alright, so what's the name?" said Arthur.

"You go first," said Josie.

"Hailie."

Josie's jaw dropped. "That's impossible."

Arthur tilted his head. "What do you mean?"

"Arthur, I was going to say Hailie too. That's the name that I've been thinking about all day."

Arthur and Josie landed at O'Hare. Arthur's sisters picked them up from the airport.

Arthur's mother and father were waiting for him in the kitchen when he walked into their house.

"Happy birthday!" they said, in near unison.

A birthday cake with twenty-seven candles, a new pair of black-and-white Vans, and a collage of Arthur's baby photos decorated the kitchen table.

Arthur ate cake, opened cards, and laughed with his family for the next hour.

"Thank you for everything," said Arthur. "I love all of you so much."

"Just continue being a good kid," said his mother.

"Keep making us proud," said his father.

Arthur and Josie went downstairs.

Josie read Margaret Atwood's *Surfacing* in bed.

Arthur eyed posters of Malcolm X, Jimi Hendrix, Thurgood Marshall, and Langston Hughes on his walls.

Arthur tweeted: "In the past year, I've gotten a book deal, become a world famous DJ, saved journalism, and my girl is pregnant. Next year is going to be wild."

Leslie texted Maggie: "Why is Arthur talking about his book? I handled that. You know he got arrested, right? The detective sent me a photo of him in the holding cell for identification. He needs to shut the fuck up."

Maggie responded: "He got arrested and he's still talking reckless? It's over. I'm sick of Arthur Simon and so is everyone else. I'm about to destroy him."

Arthur and Josie landed at LaGuardia the next night.

They took a cab to Spencer Street.

They walked out of the elevator, dropped their baggage on the hardwood floor, and fell to the couch. Josie grabbed the Xbox controller and pulled up Netflix.

"What do you want to watch?" said Josie.

"Something scary," said Arthur.

"You know I hate scary stuff," said Josie. "Let's watch a Christmas movie."

Arthur's phone got so many notifications that his battery died. He charged his phone and turned it back on.

Maggie Harvey had tweeted: "Arthur Simon put his ex-girlfriend in the hospital and dodged the bill. Stop supporting this abusive piece of shit. He lost his book deal. *Fight Women* in stores Neveruary 32nd."

Leslie Nostril posted two photos of the scar on her chin. One photo with stitches, one without. She wrote: "Arthur Simon did this to my face. Then he pitched a book and neglected to mention that he beat me."

Twitter users called Arthur a scumbag, a woman beater, and a nigger.

Voyeur published a story titled "*Abstract* Editor Leslie Nostril's Ex-Boyfriend Arthur Simon Charged With Assault, Menacing, Harassment."

Record published a story titled "Leslie Nostril Says That Arthur Simon Is An Abuser."

Backstage published a story titled "Did Rake's Best Friend Beat His Girlfriend?"

Each story had an Editor's Note stating Arthur was a friend of writers and editors at the publication.

Arthur tweeted: "Leslie Nostril is a liar, a racist, and an abuser. I have video of her saying she will lie about me hitting her and get away with it because she's white."

Twitter users called Arthur a liar, a woman beater, and a nigger.

Alexandria told Arthur to go silent.

Arthur deleted Twitter from his phone.

The Book Club canceled December shows in Toronto and Montreal.

Arthur was fired from Sounds by Surgeon Tre.

The Spencer Street apartment was listed for rent.

Arthur and Josie packed up the entire apartment and stuffed both of their cars full of moving boxes.

ELEVEN

Josie found an apartment in Ithaca.

The apartment was a beautiful two-bedroom, rented by a friend of Josie's sister, who moved out when she reached the last month of her own pregnancy.

Arthur received five thousand dollars from *Traction* for the Wolf Haley story. Josie's parents told Arthur that he could wait to pay them back. Arthur had enough savings to cover rent for three months.

Ithaca was a town of white liberals on the far left. Subarus and Volvos were status symbols. Restaurants were farm-to-table. Churches were LBGTQ-friendly.

Arthur stopped doing cocaine in Ithaca. Josie showed Arthur around her hometown and helped him rediscover life's simple pleasures.

Arthur and Josie went on movie dates every Friday night. They went to the gym. They went on nature walks and took in the small city's breathtaking gorges.

Arthur hated white liberals after they ruined his life with false accusations, but he respected Josie's mother. She led a committee that went to police stations to teach officers about implicit bias against blacks. She did not consider Twitter witch hunts a form of social justice.

Arthur became closer with his own mother.

He had never gone more than two weeks without speaking to her, but when he was in the throes of his addiction, the conversations were short. Arthur would always rush off the phone to get back to cocaine.

Arthur's mother told him to pray. He recited the Twenty-Third Psalm every morning. He took his Bible to New York City for his first court date.

The fifteenth of January was the birthday of Arthur's maternal grandmother. Arthur thought that he would waltz into the courthouse and the case would be dismissed the first time it was brought before a judge.

Arthur and Josie stayed at the Dazzler in downtown Brooklyn because it was a short walk to the courthouse. They checked in the night before court.

Josie drove into Manhattan that night and had dinner with the children she used to nanny. Arthur walked to Bedford-Stuyvesant and got a haircut on Marcy Avenue.

Arthur wanted to see Manny Rollins, but he did not want to go near Manhattan Avenue, where he might see Leslie, Maggie, or Derek.

Arthur met Josie back at the hotel. They had sex on the plush king-size bed. Arthur set three alarms for the morning. They fell asleep watching premium cable on the hotel television.

Arthur and Josie filled up on continental breakfast in the hotel lobby in the morning. Arthur wore a suit. Josie wore a dress.

They walked to the courthouse on Schermerhorn Street, through the metal detectors, and into the vomit-colored lobby where they met Alexandria.

Arthur stood before the judge for five minutes. Another court date was set for the following month.

The case was not dismissed. Arthur realized the legal battle would drag on longer than anticipated.

He and Josie left the city with no greater understanding of their fate. They bought a dozen New York bagels because the bagels in Ithaca were terrible.

Arthur figured the only way to dig himself out of the hole that he was in was to do what he knew how to best: write.

The Ithaca nights were freezing. Temperatures dipped well into the negative degrees. Arthur went without sleep on many of those nights.

He wrote a screenplay titled *Tuxedo Park*. The screenplay was about a group of wealthy teens in upstate New York and how their misadventures over Christmas vacation lead to the accidental death of a local rival.

He wrote a screenplay titled *Heteroflexible*. The screenplay was about a married couple in Los Angeles and how the husband's revelation that he wants to have sex with men leads to the dissolution of their marriage.

He wrote a pilot titled *Cuffing Season*. The pilot was about a group of drug-addicted media employees in Brooklyn and how their incestuous exploits lead to the implosion of their social circle.

Arthur completed those scripts by February and sent them to Clancy Chambers, who sent them to his wide network of Hollywood connections.

All of the scripts were rejected.

Arthur began writing a novel titled *Killer Season*.

Arthur was certain that, if his case was dismissed, he could sell the novel to Tim Goldberg.

The second court date was on the twenty-third of February, the birthday of Arthur's sister.

Arthur and Josie stayed at the Best Western in Chinatown because it was the cheapest hotel available that was a reasonable distance from the courthouse. They checked in the night before court.

They ate dinner at a Chinese restaurant and bought cannolis in Little Italy.

They went back to the hotel. Josie wanted to have sex. Arthur was too stressed out about court. He fell asleep working on the first draft of his novel.

Arthur and Josie filled up on continental breakfast in the hotel lobby the morning. Arthur wore jeans and a polo shirt. Josie wore leggings and a sweater.

Josie wanted to come to the courthouse with Arthur, but they had to drive from Chinatown to the courthouse, and parking was scarce. Josie stayed with the car while it was parked in a tow-away zone.

Arthur walked to the courthouse on Schermerhorn Street, through the metal detectors, and into the vomit-colored lobby where he met Alexandria.

Arthur stood before the judge for five minutes. Another court date was set for the following month.

The prosecutor offered Arthur a plea deal. The deal was that if Arthur pled guilty to harassment, attended therapy, and enrolled in a batterer's intervention program, the case would be dismissed, if he stayed out of trouble for the year thereafter. Arthur refused the plea deal.

He and Josie left the city with no greater understanding of their fate. They did not buy a dozen New York bagels. Arthur's savings were running dry.

Arthur wanted to kill himself.

He fantasized about drowning himself in one of the lakes surrounding Ithaca. He hated himself for corrupting Josie and Hailie's innocent lives.

Arthur had always been depressed. Cocaine was self-medication. Without cocaine, suicide enticed him. He knew the protagonist in his novel would commit suicide from the moment he began writing it.

The dark cloud passed.

Arthur was helped along by messages of support from fans. Every day, he received emails, texts, and direct messages from people who missed his writing. But fans did not pay the bills. Neither did not killing himself.

Arthur had to get a job.

The same corporations that once trotted him around as their semi-famous star employee and lavished him with six-figure salaries would not return his emails. He got a job working for his brother-in-law's construction company. He made $17.50 an hour.

Arthur was probably the only person in history to do construction work in Alexander Wang. Everything he owned was designer, but his days of purchasing eight hundred dollar Dior pants were over.

Josie's spirit never faltered. She genuinely believed love was all that she, Arthur, and the baby needed. Arthur used to have that spirit, and love was crucial to his survival, but he needed money too.

Josie made breakfast at the crack of dawn every day. She and Arthur ate eggs, bacon, and bagels.

Arthur drove forty-five minutes south on Route Thirteen to the construction site in Horseheads. He nailed and hauled wood until night.

The third court date was on the twenty-eighth of March, the day after Easter.

Josie did not join Arthur on the trip to New York because she was thirty-nine weeks pregnant.

Arthur stayed at Manny's apartment because he could not afford a hotel. He arrived the night before court.

Manny was with Ryan and Aaron at a music festival in Miami. Arthur stayed at the apartment alone.

He called Josie and told her that he made it to Manny's. He did not eat. He was full from Easter dinner.

Arthur filled up on coffee and cigarettes on Manhattan Avenue in the morning. He wore sweatpants and a T-shirt.

Arthur took the subway from Nassau Avenue to Fulton Street, got off, walked to the courthouse on Schermerhorn Street, through the metal detectors, and into the vomit-colored lobby where he met Alexandria.

Arthur stood before the judge for five minutes. Another court date was set for three months later. Trial would begin the twenty-seventh of June, Leslie's birthday.

The case entered discovery. Prosecutors handed Alexandria their paperwork.

The corroborating affidavit said that Leslie filed charges to stop Arthur from writing about her in his book.

He left the city with no greater understanding of his fate. He could barely afford the gas to make it home.

Arthur and Josie had weekly check-ins with their midwife once Josie reached full-term. They took secondhand baby clothes from Josie's three-year-old niece. They purchased a swing set and a changing table. They set up the nursery.

Arthur's check from the construction job was gone after utility payments. He and Josie went on welfare so that they could eat. They fell behind on rent. They returned aluminum cans and glass bottles to the grocery store and received six dollars.

Arthur spent his sleepless nights hunched over in the kitchen, crying, writing, dreaming of the day when he would sell his novel and save his family.

The prosecutor in Arthur's case called Leslie and asked her if she was ready to testify at trial.

Arthur got a long text from Leslie: "Look, I'm not supposed to contact you, but if you want to settle this between us, out of court, I am willing to before a trial takes over the next five years of our lives. I am disobeying the order of protection and allowing you to as well. Okay?

I just spoke to the district attorney, hence why I'm texting so late. Let me know if you'd like to talk. Arthur, I'm not out to get you. You pitched a book about me and did shitty things to me, but I never want to see a black man in jail, and I'm willing to work with you to avoid that."

Arthur walked to the bedroom. He showed Leslie's text to Josie.

"Why is she texting you?" said Josie, shaking with anger. "This ignorant bitch wants to make amends like she didn't already ruin our lives for no reason. Do not respond to her under any circumstances."

"I'm never speaking to her again," said Arthur. "I will use her guilt about trying to starve an innocent child to get the case dismissed, but that's it. She's dead to me."

"How dare she say she never wants to see a black man in jail. She already sent you to jail. She already lied to the world. She's a disgrace to women and I hope she dies."

Josie wanted to drink the tequila that had been sitting in the kitchen since New Year's Eve. She wanted to smoke one of Arthur's cigarettes. She thought of the baby and took a long, hot shower instead.

Arthur sent Leslie's text message and contact information to his lawyer in the morning.

Alexandria spoke to Leslie that afternoon and called Arthur that night.

"She wants to drop the case," said Alexandria. "But she wants you to sign a contract before she tells the prosecutor that she won't be cooperating at trial."

"What kind of contract?" said Arthur.

"She wants a mutual agreement that you will both delete your previous tweets concerning the incident. She wants you to pay her three hundred fifty dollars for her second medical bill. And she wants you to make a public apology after the case is dismissed."

"I'm not signing anything about a public apology," said Arthur. "She's the one who owes me an apology."

"Then you should start preparing for trial."

"Can we make it a two-part contract, where I only agree to make a public apology after she deletes her tweets and fulfills her part of the contract?"

"That's possible. I'll work on something with her lawyer. Her lawyer is *Abstract*'s general counsel."

Arthur's lawyer and Leslie's lawyer drew up the contract. Leslie would have to delete her tweets accusing Arthur of domestic abuse to trigger his public apology. Arthur did not believe that Leslie would delete her tweets.

They signed the contract the next day.

Arthur deleted his tweets.

He did not have any money, but Josie had four hundred sixteen dollars in her checking account because she had received cash from her grandmother as a gift.

Josie wrote a check for three hundred fifty dollars. Arthur sent it to Alexandria, who sent it to *Abstract*'s general counsel, who sent it to Leslie.

Leslie scheduled a meeting with the prosecutor in Arthur's case for the following week.

At the meeting, Leslie told the prosecutor that she wanted the charges against Arthur dropped.

The prosecutor told Leslie that the case against Arthur would be dismissed at his next court date.

TWELVE

Josie went into labor in the morning on the nineteenth of April. Arthur held Josie's hand and massaged her back during light contractions throughout the day.

When night fell, Arthur ran a water hose from the sink to the bedroom. The midwife arrived and took notes. Josie got into the birthing tub. She sipped water between contractions. Arthur massaged her neck.

Josie was too relaxed in the birthing tub and her contractions became less frequent. She and Arthur went to sleep at 2:00 a.m. Josie was jolted awake by contractions every thirty minutes. She slept in between the pain.

Josie and Arthur got out of bed at 5:30 a.m. The midwife checked Josie's cervix. She felt the baby's head at the edge of the birth canal. Josie had to dilate another seven centimeters before birth was possible.

The midwife said that Josie and Arthur could transfer to a hospital if they wanted to induce stronger contractions. Josie and Arthur wanted to stay home.

The midwife said that fear could be why Josie's labor had stalled. Josie and Arthur spent two hours in the bedroom kissing and practicing nipple stimulation.

They came out from the bedroom at 7:30 a.m. Arthur made Josie a chocolate milkshake. The chocolate milkshake disguised the taste of the castor oil.

Josie and Arthur left the apartment and went to get coffee and morning buns. They walked in the park near their apartment and waited for the labor-inducing effects of castor oil to set in. Josie's contractions came on strong when she and Arthur walked across the bridge in the park.

Arthur held Josie from behind as she hunched over in pain on the bridge while the creek ran beneath her.

They returned to the apartment. Josie was upset because she was only having contractions every seven minutes. The pain was intense and frequent, but not yet frequent enough for birth.

The baby was active, with a heart rate that signaled she was ready for life, but she was stubborn about leaving the womb for the wicked world that awaited her.

Josie and Arthur went back to bed. Josie tried to sleep, but she was uncomfortable. She shifted positions with every contraction. She squeezed Arthur's hand with all of her strength and grimaced through the pain.

The midwife went home to shower, check on her children, and sleep. She would be back in the evening.

Josie's mother, father, sisters, and niece came over with lunch at noon.

Josie started to have contractions every four minutes. The sharp, foreign pain rocking through her body hijacked conversations with her family. She squeezed Arthur's hand tighter each time.

Josie wanted to be alone with Arthur. Her family left at 3:00 p.m. She got into the birthing tub and reclined in the water while Arthur massaged her nipples.

The midwife returned an hour later and checked the baby's vitals. The baby's heart rate had accelerated.

Josie and Arthur went for another walk at 5:00 p.m. They returned to the apartment thirty minutes later.

Josie alternated between sitting on and leaning against an exercise ball. Her contractions continued to come on every four minutes.

Josie and Arthur laid in bed for the next two hours. They tried to sleep. Contractions kept Josie awake. She grabbed Arthur's hand every four minutes and kept him awake as well.

Josie got in the shower. She sipped water in between bursts of pain that caused her to grab the curtains, nearly ripping them from the rod.

When night fell again, Josie leaned over the kitchen table during five strong contractions. Arthur massaged her back. Specks of blood formed at her ankles.

The midwife checked Josie's cervix at 10:00 p.m. Josie had dilated to eight centimeters.

Josie spent the next four hours sitting, standing, walking, and kneeling during contractions. She broke out into tears and hugged Arthur tighter than she ever had. She was exhausted but heroic.

Josie and Arthur went back to bed. The midwife reached into Josie and repositioned the baby's head. She moved the baby to a position where she was better aligned to move down and out of the birth canal.

Josie was dilated to ten centimeters by 5:00 a.m. She kneeled at the side of the bed and pushed for the first time. The baby's head was finally past the cervix.

Four millimeters of the baby's head were visible at 7:00 a.m. The baby was still in her amniotic sac. Arthur saw the baby's hair swirling beyond the amniotic fluid.

Josie pushed for the next hour. She used every morsel of strength and energy she had left. She let out loud yells with each push and grabbed Arthur's arm so hard that she cut off his circulation.

More of the baby's head was visible. Arthur held up a mirror in front of Josie's vulva so that she could see the progress that she was making.

Arthur massaged Josie's nipples. Josie pushed and her face flushed bright red.

Josie let out one excruciating scream.

Hailie Jane Simon was born at 8:08 a.m. on the twenty-first of April. She weighed eight pounds and had a head full of curly black hair.

Josie was a mother. Arthur was a father.

Hailie stared into her father's eyes for eight seconds then latched onto her mother's breast.

Arthur's mother was eager to see her first grandchild and flew to Ithaca three days after Hailie was born.

Arthur's mother grew up poor on the south side of Chicago with five older brothers, one younger sister, and a single mother.

She met Arthur's father—who grew up under similar circumstances—when she was eighteen and he was twenty-one. They dated for six years, married, and had Arthur two years after the wedding.

Arthur's father was an accountant. Arthur's mother stayed at home. They raised Arthur and his two sisters in a middle class neighborhood in Chicago. Then Arthur went to school at the University of Illinois. Then he moved to New York City.

Arthur's mother was deeply in love with Hailie. She held the baby as often as possible during the week that she was in Ithaca. She cooked with one hand and held Hailie with the other. She told Arthur and Josie to move to Chicago so that she could help them raise the baby.

Arthur's father had given Arthur's mother his credit card to finance a shopping trip for baby supplies.

Arthur and his mother went to the baby store and bought bibs, bottles, clothes, blankets, books, diapers, wipes, slings, pacifiers, and toys.

Arthur and his mother returned to the apartment and unloaded the car.

"Mrs. Simon, thank you so much," said Josie.

"You're welcome," said Arthur's mother. "It's just a little something to help you get started."

Arthur and his mother left the apartment and went to get coffee. They walked in the park near Arthur's apartment and sat on a bench in front of the creek.

"Hailie is such a happy baby," said Arthur's mother, taking a sip of coffee.

"I just want her to have a good life," said Arthur.

"God didn't bring that baby into this world to have a hard life. It's going to work out for you, Arthur. I see it. I pray for you every day."

"I've been praying too."

"When is the case dismissed?"

"Two months from now, but that's just the first step. People are still going to hold this against me."

"If the case is dismissed and people still hold some drunk white girl's lies against you, fuck them."

"I agree, but *someone* needs to believe in me again, mom. I need to work. I need to feed my daughter."

"You will. You can't be discouraged. You have to get out there and tell your story. And you need to be honest about your own mistakes. You didn't hit that girl, but you were out of control and full of drugs. You never stopped to be grateful for all of the blessings that you had. Now you've been humbled. You needed that. Someone will understand. Someone will give you another chance."

"I'm writing a novel about everything. I'm going to send it to the editor who made me an offer last year. If he buys the novel, that will solve everything."

"Great. You have a gift, son. You have to use it."

"I will, but the odds are against me, mom. There are no black people in publishing. That editor is still going to look at me like I'm guilty because I'm a nigger."

"When you think like that, you've already given up. Be confident. Talk to God. Tell Him why you need this. If it's in God's plan, it will happen for you."

THIRTEEN

Arthur and Josie packed up their car, strapped their daughter into her car seat, and drove to New York City for Arthur's final court date.

Traffic was bad. The highway was a parking lot.

The heat was the worst. Stiff, humid air suffocated the vinyl interior of the car. The air conditioning was broken. Lowering the windows provided no relief.

Hailie's calm demeanor saved Arthur and Josie. She was a serene, precocious child, two months old with the neck strength and vocal ability of a five-month-old. All Hailie wanted was love, milk, and new scenery for her big brown eyes. When she had enough of the world, she slept peacefully. She slept the entire way to New York City, traffic, heat, and all.

Arthur and Josie's financial situation had improved from destitute to barely manageable.

Arthur stopped working construction when Hailie was born and stayed at home, but he was paid eight hundred dollars to write descriptive copy for a fashion startup's website. Six hundred of those dollars went to bills, but Arthur drove to New York City and felt rich.

Two hundred dollars in the checking account was better than a negative balance. It was a far cry from the days when Arthur ran to the ATM on DeKalb Avenue and made a two hundred dollar withdrawal for cocaine three times in one night, but, with two hundred dollars, he could afford gas, coffee, cigarettes, and a few meals in the city.

Arthur had also finished his novel and sent the manuscript to his agent. He held onto the hope that he would receive a positive response from the editor.

Josie made money for the family with a job she found writing news segment scripts at a local radio station. She was paid a hundred dollars per script, and completed at least two a week, so a miniscule amount of money was in Josie's checking account as well.

Josie was also the one who filled out paperwork for welfare and got the family two hundred eighty dollars a month in government assistance for groceries.

They made it work, and despite the circumstances, they were happy. Arthur was still prone to depression, but Josie was optimistic and resourceful. She cooked epic meals with the little they had. She kept the family resilient. When Arthur, Josie, and Hailie were together, in their home, at the park, on the east shore of Cayuga Lake, love was relentless. They were invincible. They survived.

The family approached the city from Palisades Parkway and saw skyscrapers reflecting sunlight across the Hudson. The city looked different to Arthur. New York was a fallen empire, a relic of a corrosive, shameful past.

Memories shot by as the car made its way up Manhattan Avenue. Beloved was closed. A sign on the door read *For Rent* in red letters reminiscent of blood.

Manny slept on his couch and left for work at the crack of dawn. When Arthur, Josie, and Hailie woke up in Manny's bed, the apartment was already empty.

Arthur went downstairs and smoked a cigarette in front of the apartment. He went to get coffee and bagels. He watched Manhattan Avenue come to life. The denizens of Brooklyn began another death march.

Arthur returned to the apartment. Josie and Hailie were dressed in rompers. Josie wanted to come to court.

"Hailie will never see the inside of a courthouse," said Arthur. "I'm going by myself."

"This is a special moment," said Josie. "I want to be there with you when this is finally over."

"Nothing happens in court. Nothing about court is special. I understand why you want to come, but it's going to be anticlimactic. I'll see you after it's done."

"What are we going to do while you're gone?"

"Stay here. Drink your coffee. Eat your bagel. I'll be back before you know it."

"Let me drive you there, at least," said Josie.

Arthur looked at the clock on Manny's stove. He was running late.

Josie dropped Arthur off in front of the courthouse on Schermerhorn Street. She gave him a kiss.

"Me and Hailie will find a restaurant to wait in around here," she said. "Good luck, baby."

"Thank you for everything," said Arthur.

The metal detector line was shorter than usual. Arthur met Alexandria in the vomit lobby for the last time.

"It's finally over," Arthur said, as the elevator ascended to the eighth floor.

"Yes, it is," said Alexandria. "Congratulations."

Arthur stood before the judge for five minutes.

"Your Honor, the People move to dismiss," said the prosecutor.

"Case dismissed," said the judge. "Temporary order of protection is vacated. Have a nice day."

Arthur and Alexandria rode the elevator back down to the first floor.

"Leslie never deleted her tweets," said Arthur. "That means I don't have to issue the apology, right?"

"That's correct," said Alexandria. "Based on the language of the contract, you are not obligated."

"Thank you. That's all I wanted to know. Now I can move on my with my life."

The elevator opened.

"You're welcome. And please pay me as soon as you can. You owe me fifteen thousand dollars."

"I'm working on it," said Arthur. "I'm supposed to hear back from the book publisher any day now."

Arthur left court and stepped onto Schermerhorn Street a free but broken man.

He won the battle, but his future was uncertain. Arthur's only concern was his daughter. He did not know how he would provide for her.

Arthur prayed for a response from the editor. He prayed Tim Goldberg would give him the same chance as before now that the case was resolved.

Arthur refreshed his inbox.

No response.

Arthur called Josie.

"Where are you?" he said.

"Two blocks away from you, on Court Street. I'm double parked at the corner with the hazards on. Hailie just had an explosion. I'm changing her diaper."

Arthur walked towards Court Street and refreshed his inbox again.

His heart nearly stopped.

Tim Goldberg had responded.

The prayer worked.

Arthur opened the email from his agent.

The email read: "I just talked to Tim. He's passing on the novel. Let's talk about it when you have a moment. Long story short, he likes the material but is really concerned about you doing this book now. His thought was that you still need some distance from the abuse scandal and that you need to do a big piece and change the narrative before any editor will be able to go to their boss and convince them to invest in you."

Rejected.

Leslie won the war.

Josie was finished changing Hailie's diaper when Arthur knocked on the window of the car.

Josie jumped out of the car and kissed Arthur in the middle of the street.

"You did it," Josie said, staring into Arthur's eyes, her arms locked behind his neck. "I'm so happy for you."

"We did it," said Arthur. "None of this would have been possible without you and Hailie."

"We should celebrate."

"There's nothing to celebrate, baby."

"Sure there is," said Josie, looking into the car to check on Hailie. "You won the case. You're free."

"I heard back from the publisher," said Arthur.

"When?"

"Just now."

"Oh my God. What happened?"

"They passed."

"What did they say?"

"The editor said I need to 'change the narrative.' Case dismissed isn't good enough when you're black. Can we leave now? I don't want to be in this city anymore."

"Of course, baby." Josie kissed Arthur again. "I'm still proud of you. We're doing everything we can. I'm ready to leave too. So is the baby."

"Let's eat an amazing lunch that we can't afford, go to Manny's, pack everything up, and go home."

"That sounds perfect. You relax. I'll drive."

Arthur got in on the passenger side of the car and turned to look at his daughter in the back seat.

"Hailie, don't ever move to New York City."

The baby cooed and let out an indecipherable yelp. She was perfectly content and gorgeous, oblivious to the grim reality surrounding her existence.

The car pulled away from Manny's apartment just as the weather started to change.

Dark clouds overtook the sunny skies. Torrential downpour consumed the Brooklyn streets. Arthur looked at the landscape in the distance as Josie drove out of the city. He saw the looming skyscrapers shrouded in fog.

Somewhere in the city, Leslie was celebrating her birthday with all of the people who had betrayed Arthur, all of the people he had introduced her to.

Arthur and Josie reached Paterson and the rain was worse. Thunderstorms and flash floods choked the pavement. Downpour obscured the windshield. The car hydroplaned when Josie switched lanes.

"We should pull over," said Arthur. "I don't know if this is safe with a baby in the car."

"I can handle it," said Josie. "I'm not worried about us. It's these other drivers that I don't trust. Like, who the fuck is this behind us with their high beams on?"

Arthur looked through the rear window and saw a white van tailgating the car. The van's headlights shot blinding silver light throughout the interior.

Arthur was staring at the ceiling when there was a sudden, loud knock at the front door followed by ghoulish laughter that shot throughout the bedroom.

Arthur looked out of the bedroom window and saw a white van parked in front of the apartment.

He was snatched from behind by a mob of hooded figures in brightly colored T-shirts.

He tried to scream out to Hailie and Josie but he had no voice. The hooded figures were strong and dragged Arthur through his front lawn to the white van.

They held Arthur down in the back of the white van while the hooded driver sped away from Ithaca. The windows were down. The sunroof was open. The air inside of the van was very cold.

The driver laughed furiously. Condensation escaped a mouth stained by a dark red liquid, maybe wine, but possibly blood. Arthur could not get a clear look.

He could only see the hooded figures holding him down against the steel floor of the van.

Arthur saw their hands and the bottoms of their faces under the leather flaps of the hoods. Their skin was orange. They laughed like the driver, exposing sets of crooked, yellow teeth.

Arthur saw the sky changing through the sunroof of the van. He saw oscillating waves of purple, blue, and red. A bright red sun rose above the landscape and disintegrated all remaining traces of night.

The hooded figures pulled Arthur into an upright position. He saw the van's dashboard. It was 3:53 a.m.

They dragged Arthur out of the van and towards a barren field with shadowy bleachers enclosing the perimeter. The driver trailed the mob, chain-smoking.

The field had an enormous entrance stand erected before it. The stand reminded Arthur of the entrance to Tivoli Gardens in Copenhagen. Another hooded figure stood in a glass box underneath the stand and handed out tickets for admission to the field.

Five hundred thousand hooded figures waited in line for tickets to enter the field. They chatted amongst themselves. The line moved rapidly. The tickets were free.

The words BLACK AMERICAN PSYCHO were lit in flickering white lights across the top of the stand.

The mob dragged Arthur past the stand. He saw the hooded figures from the line filing into the shadowy bleachers surrounding the field. There were not enough seats in the bleachers to accommodate the entire crowd, but, somehow, they kept coming.

A large oak tree with different colored branches was in the center of the field. A single tan rope hung from the tree with its knots formed into a noose.

A small stage with a podium and a microphone was next to the tree.

The driver smoked a final cigarette. The mob dragged Arthur towards the tree. The mob stopped dragging Arthur when he was directly below the noose.

The crowd in the bleachers roared.

Arthur tried to move and scream but he had no strength and no voice. The mob kept him restrained below the noose. The driver took the stage and approached the podium to deafening applause.

The driver grabbed the microphone with orange, scaly hands and spoke through the leather hood.

"We are gathered here today to observe the death of Arthur Simon," said the driver.

The crowd roared again.

"And most importantly," the driver continued, "to celebrate the essential work of our incredible, fantastic, and extremely necessary Black American Psycho unit."

The crowd roared louder. The decibel level on the field was so high that the noose shook in mid-air as it dangled from the edge of a brown tree branch.

"Colleagues, remove your hoods," said the driver. "Show yourselves to the crowd."

The mob placed Arthur in bright silver handcuffs.

They removed their hoods and revealed ugly orange faces. Their faces reminded Arthur of adversaries he had provoked over the previous three years.

The mob's facial features were grotesque and distorted. Orange scales oozed with an iridescent layer of slime. Yellow teeth caulked with decay. Red eyes matched the portentous sun in the sky.

The mob raised their fists into the air and received a thunderous standing ovation from the crowd.

The crowd chanted "Remove your hood!" while the driver stood at the podium soaking up the applause.

The driver removed its hood.

The driver was Leslie Nostril, a grotesque, distorted version with purple hair. Razor-sharp teeth were exposed when she smiled and waved at the crowd.

She waited five minutes for the applause to settle. She grabbed the microphone and addressed the crowd.

"Arthur Simon was a nigger who got out of line and thought that he was special," said Leslie. "He wrote terrible articles about white girls and celebrities. He was a fake DJ. He was arrogant. He was a cokehead, a coon, and a faggot. He never beat me, but that was obvious. Those allegations were merely the impetus for a more noble cause. Arthur Simon was a psycho and he had to go. We just needed an excuse to end him once and for all."

Ghoulish laughter rang from the bleachers. Hysterical "Hang him!" chants bellowed across the field.

Leslie waited another five minutes for silence to return. She grabbed the microphone.

"I understand your excitement," said Leslie. "But before we hang Arthur Simon, I'd like to personally thank my very dear colleague, Maggie Harvey. She was the brains behind this operation. I was merely the vessel. Maggie, please, come to the stage."

A grotesque, distorted version of Maggie Harvey left the mob, walked to the stage, and approached the podium. She smiled and waved at the ravenous, clapping crowd of nameless spectators still wearing their hoods.

Leslie patted Maggie on the back. "Maggie, please, say something to the crowd."

Maggie blushed and held one hand over her heart. She put her other arm around Leslie and leaned into the microphone. "Wow. Leslie, this is an honor. I just want to say that I appreciate the recognition, but you deserve most of the credit for the successful execution of this operation. The rest of the credit goes to the crowd. I'm talking to every single one of you in the bleachers. Thank you."

The "Hang him!" chants started again, louder and more violent than before.

"And one last thing," Maggie continued. "This is not our fault. Arthur Simon did this to himself."

Leslie slashed her left arm from high to low in a sharp vertical motion. The movement signaled to the mob restraining Arthur to lift him into the cold air.

Arthur tried to move and scream but he had no strength and no voice.

The noose tightened around his neck.

The crowd jumped out of their seats in the bleachers and rushed the field for a closer look at the lifeless body.

Arthur woke up in a cold sweat from the night terror.

He was relieved to find Josie and Hailie next to him, but the wretched visions in his mind bled into reality. The bedroom took on a surreal quality. Arthur was not certain if what occurred had necessarily been a dream.

Hailie was crying.

Josie was exhausted from driving through the storm, and awake, but groggy.

Arthur picked up Hailie.

He rocked her small, delicate body back and forth and stopped her from crying.

He took her to the changing table and changed her wet diaper. She writhed and flustered for a moment but quickly went back to sleep.

Arthur laid Hailie in the bed between himself and Josie and moved his body closer to both of them.

He stared at the ceiling and watched the patterns distort from benign to ominous figures.

There was a sudden, loud knock at the front door followed by ghoulish laughter that shot throughout the bedroom. His pulse rose. He was nervous.

Arthur looked out of the bedroom window and saw a white van parked in front of the apartment.

ABOUT THE AUTHOR

Ernest Baker is black.

34386054R00091

Made in the USA
Middletown, DE
19 August 2016